Magic Christmas

Three Books in One

SUE BENTLEY

illustrated by Angela Swan

Grosset & Dunlap

GROSSET & DUNLAP
An Imprint of Penguin Random House LLC, New York

Text copyright © 2007, 2008, 2009 by Sue Bentley. Illustrations copyright © 2007, 2008,
2009 by Angela Swan. Cover illustrations copyright © 2007, 2008, 2009 by Andrew Farley.
A Christmas Surprise first published in Great Britain in 2007 by Penguin Books Ltd., and in
the United States in 2008 by Grosset & Dunlap. *Snowy Wishes* first published in Great Britain
in 2008 by Penguin Books Ltd., and in the United States in 2013 by Grosset & Dunlap.
A Christmas Wish first published in Great Britain in 2009 by Penguin Books Ltd., and in the
United States in 2013 by Grosset & Dunlap. This bind-up edition published in 2019
by Grosset & Dunlap, an imprint of Penguin Random House LLC, New York.
GROSSET & DUNLAP is a trademark of Penguin Random House LLC.
Printed in the USA.

Visit us online at www.penguinrandomhouse.com.

The Library of Congress has cataloged the individual books under the following
Control Numbers: 2008017245, 2013025815, 2013025816.

ISBN 9780593096444   10 9 8 7 6 5 4 3 2 1

Contents

A fluffy Labrador puppy needs a friend!

Magic Puppy

Snowy
Wishes

SUE BENTLEY

To Teddy—tiny dog with a big heart

Magic Puppy

Snowy Wishes

SUE BENTLEY

illustrated by Angela Swan

Prologue

Storm rolled on his back on the stony ground. The young silver-gray wolf enjoyed the scratchy feeling against his thick fur. It felt good to be back in his homeland.

Suddenly, a fierce howl rose into the air and echoed over the quiet hillside.

"Shadow!" gasped Storm. The fierce lone wolf who had attacked Storm's

Moon-claw pack was very close. He
should have known that it wasn't safe
to return.

There was a flash of bright gold
light and a silent explosion of gold
sparks. The young wolf disappeared
and in its place stood a tiny, fluffy
white Labrador puppy with floppy
ears and big midnight-blue eyes.

Storm's short puppy legs trembled.
He needed to find somewhere to hide,
and quickly.

Halfway up the slope, thick bushes
clung to the rough ground. Storm
raced toward them, his little paws
kicking up spurts of dust. A dark wolf
shape was crouching near one of the
bushes. Storm's breath caught in his
throat with terror, and he skidded

sideways in an attempt to escape.

"In here, my son," the wolf called in a deep, gentle growl.

"Mother!" Storm yapped with relief.

He stopped and raced back toward the bush where she was hiding. As he reached her, Storm's whole body wriggled and his silky little tail wagged delightedly.

Canista reached out a huge paw and gathered her disguised pup close against her warm body. She licked Storm's fluffy white muzzle. "I am glad to see you again, but you cannot stay. Shadow is looking for you. He wants to lead the Moon-claw pack, but the others will not follow him while you live."

Storm's midnight-blue eyes sparked

with anger and fear. "He has already killed my father and brothers and wounded you. I will fight Shadow and make him leave our lands."

Canista showed her strong, sharp teeth in a proud smile. "Bravely said, but Shadow is too strong for you, and I am still weak from his poisoned bite and cannot help you. Go back to the other world. Hide there and return when you are wiser and your magic is stronger."

Storm whined softly. He knew his mother was right, but he hated to leave her.

He huffed out a warm puppy breath that glittered with a thousand tiny gold sparks. The healing mist swirled round Canista's paw and then sank into her thick gray fur.

"Thank you, Storm. The pain is much better," she rumbled softly.

Suddenly, another terrifying howl rang out and there came the sound of enormous paws thudding up the slope toward them.

"I know you are there, Storm. Let us finish this!" growled a harsh, cruel voice.

"Go now! Save yourself!" Canista urged.

Storm whimpered as he felt the power gathering inside his tiny form. Bright gold sparks ignited in his fluffy white fur. A bright gold light spread around him. And grew brighter . . .

Chapter
ONE

"Robyn, sweetheart. Are you awake?"

At the sound of her mom's voice in the doorway, Robyn Parsons sat up slowly. Her bunk was moving very slightly with the motion of the ship. From somewhere deep below her, she could hear the faint rumbling of the *Sea Princess*'s enormous engines.

"I wasn't asleep. I was just resting,"

Robyn murmured. "Uh-oh," she breathed
as her tummy gave a familiar lurch.

"Still feeling weak and wobbly?" Mrs.
Parsons said gently. "Poor old you. That's
nearly two days you've been stuck in
here."

"I know," Robyn said glumly, feeling
very down in the dumps.

She'd been looking forward to this
Christmas even more than usual.

Robyn didn't have any brothers or

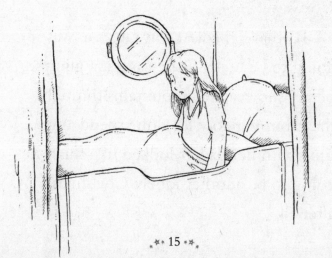

sisters, and her dad worked away from home a lot. This was the first chance in ages to spend lots of time with him, and they would all be together as a family.

"I think we deserve a vacation with guaranteed snow, lights, and lots of atmosphere! Leave it to me," Mr. Parsons had declared.

And now here they all were, all aboard the *Sea Princess* for a winter cruise around the wild and beautiful coast of Norway.

Robyn sighed. At this rate, she was going to be lucky if she caught a glimpse of any snowcapped mountains through the cabin window, let alone spend any time with her dad. It looked like this was going to be another lonely Christmas after all.

"How come you and Dad are
okay? I can barely even stand up
without wanting to throw up," she
grumbled.

"It's just sheer bad luck," her mom
said sympathetically. "We had no idea

that you'd react so badly to a sea voyage,
or we'd have chosen a different way of
spending Christmas." She handed Robyn
a glass. "Have a drink of water.
It might help."

Robyn sipped the water. She felt
a tiny bit better after having a drink.
"Thanks, Mom. I think I might stay
sitting up. Maybe I'll look through that
music magazine you got me. Where's
Dad?"

"In the sun lounge, reading his paper.
Are you sure you wouldn't like me to
bring you something? Maybe a sandwich
or some fruit?"

At the thought of food, Robyn made
a face. "I couldn't eat a thing."

Mrs. Parsons shook her head slowly.
"I'm really starting to wonder whether

we shouldn't get off the ship at the
next port and arrange to take you home."

"No! You can't!" Robyn said at once
and then wished that she hadn't spoken
so loudly. Her head felt as if it was
spinning. "Dad will be so disappointed
if we waste this vacation. And you've
been really looking forward to it for
ages."

"So have you, sweetheart," her mom
reminded her gently. "This was supposed
to be a really special Christmas together,
remember?"

Robyn nodded. "I know, but we'll
have lots more of them," she said, trying
hard to hide her disappointment for her
mom's sake. "I don't see why you and
Dad can't still have a good time. I'll be
fine in here by myself. I'm nearly ten

years old, aren't I? And I *have* to start feeling better soon. No one stays seasick forever!"

Mrs. Parsons shook her head slowly. "I'm still not happy about leaving you alone. I'm just going to pop back to have a word with your dad. Let's see what he has to say about this. I won't be long."

Robyn's shoulders slumped as the cabin door closed. Even though it wasn't her fault that she felt so ill, she knew she'd feel really guilty if their cruise was cut short.

It's just not fair! I'm so fed up of being sick! she grumbled to herself.

She took a deep breath and decided to get up. Maybe her mom and dad would change their minds about taking her home if she could convince them that she was feeling stronger.

Pushing back her quilt, Robyn slowly swung her legs over the side of her bunk. Her head swam a bit, but she stood up determinedly and reached for her jeans and fleece top. She was a bit wobbly on her feet, but she took her time getting dressed and finally managed it okay.

I'm much better. I'm fine, she told herself determinedly as she bent down to pull on her sneakers. Suddenly, a strong dizzy feeling washed over her, and she lost her balance.

"Oh," Robyn gasped, toppling forward.

She threw out her arms, ready for a painful bruising landing, when a brilliant golden flash and a shower of sparks lit up the small cabin. Time

seemed to stand still and a warm tingling
sensation ran down Robyn's spine. She
felt a sudden jolt, but there was no hard
landing.

To her complete astonishment,
Robyn found herself sprawled full-length
on her tummy on a sort of bouncy
raft, made of shimmering gold-colored
bubbles, and whizzing all around her was

an ice storm of spinning, glittering sparks.

Robyn caught her breath as she felt herself slowly rising up into a sitting position and then being lowered gently on to the floor. The bubble raft and sparks dissolved with a loud crackling noise, like chip bags being crumpled up.

Robyn sat there shakily on the floor and looked around nervously.

What had just happened? She felt like pinching herself to see if she had been dreaming.

"I hope you are not hurt," woofed a strange little voice.

Robyn nearly jumped out of her skin. "Who said that?" She twisted around, her eyes searching the small cabin.

Crouching on top of the neat chest of drawers opposite, Robyn saw a tiny, fluffy white puppy, with cute floppy ears, a silky white tail, and midnight-blue eyes. Thousands of tiny diamond-bright golden sparkles glittered in its thick fur.

Chapter
TWO

Robyn's eyes widened. Her mom must
have brought in the cute toy to cheer her
up and then forgotten to tell her about
it. She must be more affected by her
seasickness than she'd realized—first she'd
imagined floating on a sparkly bubble raft,
and now she thought she'd heard this toy
puppy speak to her!

Robyn stood up and went to reach

out toward the toy. "Hello. Aren't you gorgeous? I wonder where Mom found you."

"I came here by myself," the puppy woofed. "When you fell, I used my magic to stop you from being hurt. I am sorry if I startled you."

Robyn gasped and pulled her hand back as if it had been burned. "You . . . you *can* talk!" she cried.

The puppy blinked up at her with wide midnight-blue eyes. Despite its tiny size, it didn't seem to be afraid of her.

"Yes. I am Storm of the Moon-claw pack.
What is your name? And what is this
strange moving place?"

"Robyn. Robyn Parsons. And we're
on a ship called *Sea Princess*. I'm here on a
Christmas cruise with my parents," Robyn
explained, her mind still whirling. She
found it difficult to take all this in, but she
didn't want to scare the amazing puppy
away. "Um . . . I don't know what you
did just now, but thanks for helping me. I
could have hurt myself badly."

"You are welcome," Storm yapped.

Robyn slowly backed up to the edge
of her bunk and then sat down. "Sorry,
I'm feeling a bit sick. I've been like this
since we came on board."

Storm's little pointed face clouded
with concern. "I will make you better."

Robyn instantly felt another warm
tingling sensation down her back as
Storm reached out one fluffy, little
white paw and sent a fountain of tiny
sparks toward her. They whirled around
her, humming like tiny worker bees
before disappearing. She felt the sickness
washing downward and draining out of
her toes, just as if she'd been standing
under the flow of a warm shower.

"Wow! That's amazing," she cried
delightedly, jumping up. "I don't feel sick
anymore, and I'm not dizzy or anything!
Thanks again, Storm!"

"That is good." Storm grinned,
showing his sharp little teeth, and then
his face took on a serious expression. "I
need to hide now, Robyn. Can you help
me?"

"I'd love to, but why do you need to do that?" Robyn asked, looking down at the cute white puppy, who was beginning to tremble all over.

Storm's midnight-blue eyes darkened with anger. "An evil lone wolf attacked our Moon-claw pack—he is called Shadow. Shadow killed my father and brothers and wounded my mother. He wants to lead our pack, but the others are waiting for me."

"But how can you lead a wolf pack? You're a tiny pu–" Robyn began.

"Stand back, please!" Storm interrupted.

There was a dazzling flare of golden light, which blinded Robyn for a moment. For a second or two, she couldn't see anything. But when her

sight cleared, the cute white puppy had
gone and in its place a magnificent young
silver-gray wolf stood proudly, almost
filling the whole of the tiny cabin. Its
thick neck-ruff glittered all over as if it
had been dipped in gold dust.

Robyn caught her breath and would
have backed away if there had been
room. "Storm?" she gasped, eyeing the

young wolf's sharp teeth, strong muscles, and huge powerful paws.

"Yes, it is me. Do not be afraid. I will not harm you," Storm replied in a deep, velvety growl.

Robyn had hardly got used to the great majestic wolf when there was a final flash of dazzling light. A shower of bright sparks crackled harmlessly down around her and Storm reappeared as a cute, fluffy white puppy.

"Wow! You really are a wolf! That's an amazing disguise," Robyn whispered.

Storm tucked his little white tail between his legs, and Robyn saw that he was beginning to tremble again. "Shadow will recognize me if he finds out I'm here, and then he will use his magic against me. Please will you help?"

Robyn's soft heart went out to the tiny scared puppy. She bent down and stroked his soft little head. Storm was impressive as his real self, but in his cute puppy disguise he was totally adorable.

"Of course I'll help you and—" Robyn stopped as she realized something. "Oh, I don't think animals are allowed on board. I could try to hide you in my cabin, but it's small and you'll be really bored if you have to stay in there for the whole time."

"I can come everywhere with you. I will use my magic so that only you can see and hear me," Storm woofed eagerly. A couple of tiny sparks danced around his floppy white ears and then blinked out. "It is done."

"You've made yourself invisible?

Cool!" Robyn said delightedly. She picked
Storm up and gave him a cuddle. His
white fur was thick and silky and smelled
of cold fresh air. "Let's go and explore *Sea
Princess* together!"

"I would like that!" Storm's little white muzzle wrinkled in a smile, and he licked her chin with his pink tongue.

"I can't wait to go and find Mom and Dad and tell them about you." Robyn smiled down at him.

"No!" Storm's face was suddenly serious. "You can never tell anyone my secret. Promise me," he woofed gently.

Robyn felt disappointed that she couldn't share the news about her wonderful new friend with her parents— she was sure they would love him, too. But if it would help to keep the tiny puppy safe, Robyn decided to keep this secret to herself.

"Okay. I won't say anything. Cross my heart."

"What's this promise you're making?"

said Mr. Parsons, coming into the cabin.

"Dad!" Robyn whirled around in shock to see her mom and dad standing there. She'd been so busy talking to Storm that she hadn't heard the cabin door open. "I was just promising . . . um . . . myself," she said, thinking quickly. "That I was . . . um . . . going to have the best time ever, now that I feel better. Because I've got lots of time to make up, haven't I?"

"You certainly have," her dad said, looking surprised but delighted. "Well, I must say that you seem to have made a miracle recovery. And there your mom was, wondering whether we ought to take you home!"

Robyn still couldn't quite believe that her mom and dad hadn't noticed Storm in her arms. But when neither of them said anything about the tiny puppy, she felt herself starting to relax.

"No one's going home. So there!" Robyn exclaimed, her eyes shining.

She spun around and pretended to straighten her quilt, giving Storm the chance to jump onto her bunk.

When Robyn turned back to her

parents, her mom was beaming at her.
"I can hardly believe it. You're like a totally
different girl than the one I was talking
to just a few minutes ago. It's just like
magic!"

If only Mom knew how right she was,
Robyn thought, smiling inwardly.

"Well, you look ready to leave the
cabin at last. I expect you'd like a look
around to see what you've been missing.
Where do you feel like going?" her
dad asked.

Robyn's tummy rumbled, and she
realized that she was starving.

"Lunch it is, then!" said her mom.

As Robyn followed her parents
to an upper deck, Storm trotted invisibly
at her heel. Robyn had a warm glow
inside. After a false start, her vacation

was just beginning, and she now had a
wonderful new friend to share it with, too.

Chapter
THREE

"Doesn't everywhere look great?"
Robyn said to Storm. "It makes me feel all
Christmassy."

They were walking across a part of the
ship with a domed ceiling and
large picture windows, swathed with
evergreen garlands. Lanterns and
traditional decorations made of wood
and tin were strung around the walls

and Christmas trees gleamed with
hundreds of twinkly lights.

Robyn peered through one of the
large windows. The Norwegian sky was
filled with a strange dark-gray light and
the heavy, rolling sea looked like a sheet of
ridged silver.

"It's really weird to think that it never
gets completely light during the day in
winter. I don't know if I'd like to live here
all year round," she whispered to Storm.
"But it looks amazing, doesn't it? Like
something out of a fairy tale. You can just
imagine scaly monsters in the sea and

fierce trolls and frost giants living in the mountains."

"Trolls and frost giants?" Storm flattened his ears and his silky white tail drooped.

Robyn grinned. "Sorry. I didn't mean to scare you. I read about Viking legends and stuff when I knew we were coming here on vacation."

Storm still seemed unsure about being aboard a ship. He reared up on to his back legs beside her and pressed his little nose to the window. His big midnight-blue eyes widened, and he gave a worried little whine.

"Are you okay?" Robyn asked, wishing she hadn't mentioned giants and trolls now. She hadn't realized that Storm would take her seriously.

"I think we are lost," Storm woofed. "There is so much gray water and sky, but I cannot see any land."

"That's because we're looking out on to open sea on this side," Robyn explained. "We can go up on deck, if you like, and then you'll be able to see land and mountains."

Storm nodded, still not looking entirely happy as he jumped back down.

Robyn didn't expect that any of the magical wolves from the Moon-claw pack had ever been on a cruise ship; or on any other kind of ship for that matter. In his home world, Storm never left land. No wonder he was ill at ease.

"Come on, let's catch up with Mom and Dad," she said to Storm, changing the subject. "I could eat a horse!"

Storm's face showed surprise. "A horse? I have seen one of those. It was very large!"

"I know. I wouldn't really want to eat one. It's just something that people say when they're really hungry!"

Storm's little white muzzle twitched in a grin. Robyn was pleased to see that his anxious look had completely disappeared.

"I am very hungry, too!" he yapped, falling into step with Robyn as she set off again.

A buzz of conversation and a riot of delicious smells greeted them as they entered the restaurant. Robyn could see her mom and dad beginning to help themselves from the buffet area. She picked up a tray and joined them.

"Wow! Look at all this!" she whispered to Storm, her mouth watering. "I hardly know what to choose."

There was an enormous display of food with hot and cold dishes of all kinds, salads, sandwiches, desserts, cakes,

and baskets of fruit and chocolates. In
the center there was an entire miniature
village made of iced gingerbread and
an amazing ice sculpture of a polar bear.

Robyn heaped her plate with food
for her and Storm, and then followed
her mom and dad to an empty table.
As soon as she sat down, Storm jumped
up on to her lap and curled up.

After almost two days of just drinking
water, Robyn ate hungrily. She slipped
bits of meat and fish under the table
to Storm without her mom and dad
noticing.

"Human food tastes very good,"
Storm woofed, licking his chops when
he'd finished. "Thank you, Robyn."

Robyn's mom and dad were
wondering what to do next. "We could

go swimming or watch a movie or even
have a sauna," her mom said. "There's a
game room, shops, an Internet café, and
lots of organized events, too."

"Could we go up on deck and look
at the view?" Robyn asked. If Storm
could see that they weren't far from land,
he might feel less nervous about being on
Sea Princess.

"Fine by me," her mom said. "I think
we should be steaming through a fjord by
now. It should be quite spectacular."

Up on deck a cold wind was blowing,
and Robyn wrapped her coat around
Storm to keep him warm. The tiny
puppy was peeping out from the front
opening and Robyn could feel him
snuggled against her chest, like a fluffy
hot-water bottle.

Sea Princess was moving up a wide
channel that had been created thousands
of years ago by melting glaciers. The
fjord stretched deep into the surrounding
mountains. Painted wooden houses
were clustered on the slopes and the
towering, snowcapped tops were hidden
by clouds.

Some people sat on deck in chairs,
bundled up in warm blankets as they
enjoyed the dramatic scenery. Others
were lining the ship's rail, pointing
out details to each other and taking
photographs.

Robyn found a place to stand at the
rail and looked down at the gray-green
water, far below. "I wonder how deep it is
here," she commented to Storm.

"Some of these fjords are almost four

thousand feet deep," her dad said, coming to stand beside her. "That's as deep as the mountains you can see."

Robyn realized that she must have spoken more loudly than she'd intended to, and her dad had thought she was speaking to him. She would have to be more careful about keeping Storm's secret.

"That's scarily deep," she said to her dad.

Some way further on, the ship slowly rounded a bend and Robyn saw a waterfall gushing from a gorge in a high cliff. Jagged icicles, like spears, hung down from the rock and the foaming curtain of water fell straight down between them.

"Warm enough, honey?" her dad asked cheerfully. "This icy air's really bringing the color back to your cheeks."

"I feel fine. I don't mind the cold that much," Robyn said, giving her dad a hug. Storm gave a little warning squeak as he got a bit squashed between the two of them. "Sorry!" Robyn whispered to him, when her dad broke away.

"Well, I've had enough of it for now,"

her mom said with a shiver. "I think I
might have a sauna to warm me up."

"That's a good idea. I'll come with
you. What about you, Robyn?" her dad
asked.

Robyn shook her head. "No,
thanks." She didn't like all that hot
steam, and she didn't want to leave
Storm by himself. "I think I'll stay out
here for a while. I'll come and meet you
at the fitness center."

"All right, honey," her mom said.
"By the way, the ship's docking at a
fairly big town this afternoon. I thought
we could all go ashore and do some
shopping."

"Sounds great. Enjoy your sauna.
See you later," Robyn called as her
parents walked away. Now that she felt

well enough to spend some time with her mom and dad, she definitely didn't mind wandering around by herself with Storm.

Her dad looked over his shoulder and winked at her. "Watch out for trolls."

Robyn grinned. "I will!"

She didn't notice Storm shrinking further down inside her coat, his dewy eyes looking around nervously.

The fjord began to get narrower and more winding. The sides of the mountains were steeper here, without any houses or farms. Ice and snow clung to the jagged black rock face and the gray clouds seemed lower.

Robyn was quite enjoying the gloomy landscape. It was easy to believe that fierce trolls lay in wait for unwary travelers.

Suddenly, a bloodcurdling cry rang out
behind her. Robyn almost jumped out
of her skin, and Storm yelped in terror.
Robyn whipped around to see a number
of hairy men with huge teeth, pointed
ears, and lumpy faces running toward
her across the deck. They were dressed in
rough fur cloaks and shaking their fists.

"Trolls!" gasped Robyn.

Storm growled, his whole body
tensing inside Robyn's coat.

Robyn's heart beat fast. Some of the
other passengers screamed and one little
girl hid behind her dad.

And then Robyn saw one of the
"trolls" adjusting his mask and another
one of them straightening his hairy
wig. It was just some of the ship's crew
who had dressed up to put on a special

performance for the passengers.

She started to laugh. "It's okay, Storm. It's only . . . ," she began in a reassuring voice, but it was too late.

Robyn felt a familiar, warm prickling sensation down her spine as big gold sparks flowered in Storm's fluffy white fur and his ears crackled with magical power.

Something very strange was about to happen.

Chapter
FOUR

Robyn watched in complete
amazement as Storm leaped out of her
coat and sprang on to the deck, trailing a
comet's tail of gold sparks.

He lifted one tiny front paw and sent a
huge spray of glittering sparks whooshing
into the icy air. Robyn saw them hang
there for a second and then transform into
grayish smoke, which sank down on to

the trolls in the thickest mist she had ever seen.

"Hey! What's going on?" one of them cried from the middle of the dense mist.

"Oops, sorry," said another one, as he tripped over his friend.

They couldn't see where they were going. Robyn could hear the disguised crew members staggering around and bumping into each other. The other passengers thought it was all part of the

act and began laughing and cheering them on.

But as the magical mist spread, they became swallowed up in it, too.

"Follow me, Robyn! I will save you from the monsters," Storm yapped. His little form glowed as brightly as a lantern as he scampered toward the door to the lower deck.

"Come back, Storm!" Robyn called to him above all the noise. "They're not real trolls. They're people dressed up. It's just for fun!"

Storm stopped dead and then padded back toward her. In the little pool of light made by his magically glowing body, Robyn could see a shamefaced expression creep over his fluffy white face.

"I am sorry. I thought that you were in danger," Storm yapped quietly, flattening his ears.

"It's okay. I know you were only trying to protect me, but I think you'd better make the fog disappear now," she said gently.

Storm nodded.

He sent a big spurt of bright gold sparks whooshing across the deck. The sparkles were like a powerful jet spray at a car wash, magically blasting the fog into thin strands. Seconds later it all blew away on the icy wind.

The disguised crewmen stood there on the clear deck, looking puzzled. Their wigs were all crooked and their troll masks were dangling around their necks. But they soon recovered.

Straightening their costumes, they
skipped around the deck, roaring and
waving their arms.

Delighted applause broke out as
more of the crew came on to the deck,
holding trays of hot drinks, food, and
snacks.

"You must pay the price for entering
our land," one of the trolls boomed,
grinning broadly. "We order you to
feast with us on troll brew and hot troll
soup!"

As everyone began helping
themselves, Robyn decided that this was
a good time for her and Storm to make
their exit.

Later that afternoon after *Sea Princess*
docked at the harbor, Robyn, Storm

and her mom and dad went ashore. They
caught a bus to the south of the city with
lots of other people on the cruise.

Robyn sat with Storm safely inside
the shoulder bag on her lap. He stuck
his head out to look at the broad, snow-
covered streets and modern shops and
offices.

Robyn could see colored lights
gleaming from house windows, and
there were lots of green wreaths hung

on doors. Here and there, they passed traditional wooden buildings, painted in shades of red, orange, or mustard.

"Everything looks so Christmassy here. I love it," she whispered. "I hope I can get some presents for Mom and Dad."

Storm twisted round and looked up at her. "What is Christmas?"

"Oh, of course. I don't suppose you have it in your world, do you?" Robyn realized. "Christmas is a special time when we celebrate the baby Jesus being born. We sing carols, and families all get together and exchange presents and eat lots of yummy food. Dad usually stuffs himself with turkey, stuffing, and pie and then moans about his pants being tight! At least, that's what we usually do at home. It's going to seem a bit different this year. We celebrate Christmas on Christmas Eve aboard *Sea Princess*."

Storm looked a bit puzzled, but his midnight-blue eyes were twinkling with excitement. "It sounds very odd, but I think I will enjoy Christmas, especially the food!"

The bus stopped near an enormous cathedral with a towering spire and lots of amazing stone carving. Colored light streamed out on to the snow from its stained-glass windows.

Robyn's mom produced a tourist brochure she'd picked up on the way to the bus. "I think I'd like to look around inside that cathedral. It says here that it's almost a thousand years old. Imagine that!" she said enthusiastically.

"Wow!" Robyn said. She couldn't
imagine anything being that old. But she
didn't really want to walk around some
musty-smelling old cathedral for hours,
however impressive it was. "Do we all have

to go?" she asked, without enthusiasm.

Mr. Parsons smiled. "I don't think so. I'm not as interested in old buildings as your mom. You and I'll go shopping and meet her later."

"Oh good," Robyn said, relieved.

"Fine," Mrs. Parsons said. "I'm quite happy to wander by myself." She turned to her husband. "I'll see you back here in a couple of hours?"

Mr. Parsons nodded. "Sounds good."

Robyn waved to her mum as she set off toward the cathedral, and then she and her dad set off in search of interesting shops. Storm leaned up and hooked his front paws over her shoulder bag, so that he could look at the surroundings.

They had been walking for a couple of minutes when Storm reached out and tapped Robyn's arm with one front paw. She looked down to see that he'd pricked up his little ears.

"I can hear music," he yapped.

"I can, too," Robyn whispered. "Can you hear that, Dad?" she said in a louder voice. "It's coming from over there."

Mr. Parsons listened. "Oh yes. It's quite faint, but it sounds like folk music. Let's go and have a look."

As they walked to the end of the street, the music got louder. They reached a cobbled square, surrounded by stalls heaped with crystallized fruit, gingerbread, and spiced cookies. Cheery lanterns were strung between the buildings encircling the small square, and green garlands and decorations were looped between the stalls.

Storm yipped excitedly as he saw the bandstand, with musicians playing violins. Women in colorful felt skirts and men in vests and buckled shoes were dancing. A festive smell of spiced wine and roasted nuts filled the frosty air.

"Oh, it's a Christmas festival!" Robyn exclaimed delightedly.

Chapter
FIVE

Robyn sipped a cup of hot spiced apple juice as she watched some children building snowmen. It was a competition, and a number of half-built snow trolls and elves stood in one corner of the square. There was even a Santa Claus snowman with his snow reindeer.

In the strange half-light, the glowing lanterns cast a cheerful glow over

everything. Storm jumped out of Robyn's
bag in another little flurry of sparks.

At first, Robyn was worried that his
little paws would get cold on the frozen
ground. But Storm's white ears sizzled
with tiny sparks, and she noticed that he
was now wearing four tiny furry boots.

He looked so cute wearing them
that Robyn burst out laughing, which
she quickly turned into a cough. She

didn't want to hurt her puppy friend's feelings.

As she and her dad wandered around the market stalls, they bought cheese, chocolate, and spice cakes for presents to take home for Gran and Gramps. Robyn didn't see anything she wanted to buy for her mom and dad.

She spotted a shop on the other side of the square. "I'm just going to head over to that shop over there. I won't be long," she told her dad.

Mr. Parsons nodded. "All right. I'll still be here."

Storm scampered after Robyn as she headed across the square. Inside the shop, it felt really warm after the cold outside. Robyn took off her hat and gloves and stuffed them in her coat pocket.

There were lots of people looking at the gifts and cuddly toys. Robyn noticed a rack of knitwear. Maybe her mom would like a traditional hand-knitted cardigan.

As she went to have a closer look, Robyn heard raised voices. A sales assistant was speaking sharply to a tall, slim girl with black hair, who looked about twelve years old.

"I am not a thief!" the girl said in a low, angry voice. She was wearing a red felt skirt, decorated with bands of embroidery, and sturdy leather boots.

"We'll see about that!" the sales assistant shouted, beckoning to a man from another counter.

As Robyn stood at the far end of the long clothes rack, the man hurried over.

"What's the problem?" he asked the assistant.

"This young lady has taken an expensive *lusekofte*. See, there is the empty hanger," the woman said crossly, pointing to the rack of knitted sweaters. "I demand that she opens her bag so that I can search it!"

"Did you see her take it?" the man asked.

The woman put her hands on her hips. "No. But she must have. One's missing, and it was there a minute ago!"

"I told you. I have not taken it. I would never do that," the girl said calmly, clutching her bag with two hands.

Her face was pale, expect for her cheeks, which were flushed a deep red.

Robyn could see that the girl looked
close to tears and admired the way she
was sticking up for herself against the
bossy assistant.

"That woman's determined to
search the girl's bag. I hope she hasn't
stolen anything," Robyn whispered to
Storm.

Suddenly, Storm's head came up,
and he gave a triumphant woof.

Diving beneath the rack of sweaters,
the tiny puppy jumped up and hunted
around. He grabbed something and a
loose sweater came free. Storm dropped
it on to the floor before padding back
to Robyn.

"Oh, well done, Storm!" Robyn
praised him, pleased that it looked like
the young girl hadn't taken anything.
"The sweater must have slipped off
its hanger. It was lucky you spotted a
bit of its dangling sleeve, Storm." The
sales assistant obviously hadn't looked

carefully enough.

On impulse, Robyn picked up the empty hanger and stepped forward. "Excuse me," she said politely, holding it up. "Are you looking for the sweater that was on this?"

The two assistants and the dark-haired girl turned to look at her.

"I know where it is," the woman snapped. "It's inside this young person's bag!"

"Are you sure?" Robyn asked. "Because there's one on the floor. Look."

The assistant frowned and went to investigate. A deep flush crept up her face as she came back holding the cardigan. "I . . . er . . . seem to have made a mistake. We'll say no more about it," she said shortly. Snatching the empty hanger from Robyn, she marched briskly away.

The male assistant threw the girl an apologetic look and then hurried back to his counter.

Robyn's eyes widened. "What nerve! That woman didn't even say sorry!"

"It does not matter," the girl replied,

shrugging. "I knew I had done nothing, but thank you for speaking up for me. I am Kristiana Magga. Everyone calls me Krista. What is your name?"

"Robyn. Robyn Parsons. I'm here on vacation with my mom and dad," Robyn said, surprised that the girl was so calm after the unpleasant scene. She saw that Krista had high cheekbones and unusual dark eyes, which were slightly tilted at the corners.

"I am very glad to meet you," Krista said with a wide smile.

"Me too," Robyn said. "Do you live here?"

Krista shook her head. "I am visiting friends. My Uncle Nikolai and Aunt Jorun are with me. Oh, here they are now."

A man and woman came toward them. Robyn saw that they had high cheekbones and dark hair, like Krista. Krista's aunt also wore a blue felt skirt and strong leather boots. There was a fringed gold shawl around her shoulders, pinned with a circular brooch.

"This is my new friend Robyn," Krista said.

Robyn glowed at Krista's description of her as a friend. Since they'd only just met, it was a nice thing to do.

Krista then told her aunt and uncle about the sales assistant who had accused her of stealing. ". . . and Robyn proved that I didn't steal it after she found the *lusekofte* on the floor," she finished.

It wasn't me, actually, it was Storm, Robyn thought, wishing that she could

tell them all how fantastic her magic
friend was. She smiled proudly at the little
puppy who was sitting nearby watching,
visible only to her.

"Thank you, Robyn," Krista's aunt
said. "It's very nice to meet you. I wish we
had more time to talk, but now we must
go."

"Yes. We have many things to buy before we return to our home in the north," said her uncle.

"Good-bye, Robyn," Krista said with a warm smile. "Enjoy your vacation."

"Thanks, I will. Bye, Krista," Robyn said.

She and Storm watched as the girl and her aunt and uncle left the shop. As they walked past the glass storefront, Krista paused to wave.

Robyn waved back, feeling a little sad that she had to leave so soon. "Krista seemed really nice, didn't she?" she said to Storm. "What a shame that we'll never see her again."

"I liked her, too," Storm woofed.

"Come on, Storm. Let's go and find

Dad." She no longer wanted to buy any presents from this shop.

Chapter
SIX

The next day passed quickly. *Sea Princess* sailed along through ever more majestic fjords, and Robyn and Storm stood on deck to watch the spectacular scenery passing by. When the ship docked at another coastal town, they went ashore with her parents to explore.

Before boarding again, she found time to dash into a shop and buy her mom some traditional hand-knitted gloves. She also bought her dad a wallet and got felt slippers for her gran and gramps. "Great. I'm finished with my present-buying." *Except for Storm*, she thought, wondering how she was going to buy him a present without him seeing.

Later on Robyn, Storm, and her mom and dad sat in a cafe near the harbor.

Robyn stirred a blob of whipped cream into her mug of hot chocolate and then took a big sip. "*Mmm.* Delicious," she murmured, licking her lips.

Her dad grinned around a mouthful of muffin. "I'm not sure a chocolate mustache is a good look on you!"

"Ha-ha! Very funny." Robyn made a

face at him and wiped her mouth.

She scooped up a big fingerful of whipped cream and slipped it inside her shoulder bag for Storm to lick. His warm little tongue flicked over her fingers, and she hid a fond smile. She loved having Storm as her friend and sharing this wonderful vacation with him.

Robyn gazed out of the window as she nibbled a spice cookie and found herself thinking about Krista.

Robyn had told her mom and dad

about the sweater incident in the shop and described Krista and Jorun's beautiful clothes. "Your young friend is probably from a Sami background," her mom guessed. "I read in our travel guide that the Sami people used to be known as Lapps and once moved around with their herds of reindeer. A lot of them live a more settled life now."

Robyn remembered that Krista's Aunt Jorun had said they were returning to their home in the north. She thought it must be amazing to live in a land of ice and snow, where it got so cold that even the sea froze.

Sea Princess docked at a small port the next morning and Robyn, Storm, and her parents made their way to a smaller boat, which was waiting to take them to see a large glacier.

Passengers piled into the boat and lined the rails. Robyn looked down into the dark, freezing water, which was so much closer to them on this small boat, and shivered. It looked very cold and very scary—she held on to the boat rail as it set off. On the way to the ice cap, the vast, frozen expanse that stretched its arms down into a number of deep valleys, they sailed between islets and skerries.

Robyn was waiting excitedly for her first-ever glimpse of a glacier.

"We should see it in a minute," she whispered to Storm, who was in her shoulder bag.

Storm nodded.

Robyn was unprepared for the amazing sight that met her eyes. The frozen river, cutting through the huge snowcapped mountains, ended in a breathtaking wall of towering ice, which was reflected in the sea.

"Oh my gosh!" Robyn's jaw dropped. "That's awesome!"

Sounds of cracking, like pistol shots, rang out in the still air and some of the passengers looked worried. Storm whimpered, and Robyn glanced down to where he sat with his front paws looped over the bag. He was twitching his ears nervously.

"That noise is just the sound of boulders getting crunched under the ice," the guide explained to the worried passengers.

"Did you hear what that man said? It's nothing to be scared about," Robyn whispered reassuringly to Storm. But when he continued to stare at the glacier intently, she frowned. "Storm? Did you hear me?"

There was an extra loud *bang!* and an ominous grinding sound—Storm's

entire fluffy white body tensed, and
his hackles rose along his back. "There
is great danger!" he barked urgently,
leaping down on to the deck.

Robyn felt a familiar warm
prickling flow down her spine as big
golden sparks bloomed in Storm's fluffy
white fur and his ears sparked with
electricity. Suddenly, the little boat shot
forward in a dazzling burst of speed.

Robyn grabbed hold of the rail
again and clung on for dear life.

Storm whimpered as his claws
skittered across the deck, and he slid
toward the rail, about to fall overboard
into the freezing, bottomless sea.

Robyn acted without thinking.
Still hanging on with one hand, she
swooped down and reached out.

For one heart-stopping moment,
she thought she had lost Storm. But
then her fingers closed on the scruff
of his neck. Yes! Robyn hauled the
terrified puppy to safety and tucked his
trembling little form safely back inside
her bag.

"Thank you for saving me, Robyn!"

Storm barked, looking up at her gratefully with his big blue eyes.

"I'm just glad you're okay," she replied, trying to stay on her feet and steady her shoulder bag at the same time.

The other passengers were bracing themselves as best they could as the small boat suddenly zoomed back out to sea in a shower of golden sparkles before stopping abruptly near one of the small islets.

"Storm! What's going on?" Robyn asked in a shaky voice.

Suddenly, there was a thunderous cracking sound, and massive slabs of ice parted from the glacier and dropped into the sea with a resounding *splash!* To everyone's horror, a huge tidal wave began rushing toward the boat.

Robyn felt the color drain from her face as the wall of water bore down on them with the speed of an express train.

Storm calmly lifted both front paws and sent another fountain of sparks whooshing across the sea at the tidal wave, which immediately sank without a trace. The small boat rocked gently as normal-sized waves brushed harmlessly against its sides.

No one else could have seen Storm's magic, and the stunned passengers all began speaking at once.

Robyn looked down fondly at her little friend. "You were amazing, Storm! We could all have been really badly hurt, and you nearly were. Thank you."

Storm gave a little shake as every last spark faded from his thick fur. "I am glad I was able to help."

"Are you all right, honey?" asked Robyn's dad, putting his arm around her shoulders. "I'm a bit shaken up myself!"

"I'm fine now," Robyn said.

Beside them, Robyn's mom shuddered. "I dread to think what would have happened if we'd been right under

the glacier when that sheet of ice fell off! Thank goodness the captain had the presence of mind to put on a burst of speed."

"Whoever was responsible for saving us was very brave, wasn't he?" Robyn said meaningfully, reaching one hand into her bag to stroke Storm's warm fur.

She felt so proud of her friend. It was just a shame that no one else would ever know how wonderful he was.

Chapter
SEVEN

Robyn stood on deck, bathed in the
night's moonlight, with Storm cuddled
in her arms inside her coat. She was still a
little nervous after saving Storm the other
day and was determined to keep her little
friend safe.

It had grown colder as *Sea Princess*
steamed further north, and this was
the coldest weather Robyn had ever

experienced. The icy air prickled inside
her nose as she breathed in. It was a
strange sensation.

Storm's ears were pricked up, and his
breath fogged in the air as he gazed up
at the millions of silver stars that seemed
so close you could reach out and touch
them.

"*Brrr!*" Robyn said, trying to hide a
shiver. She was thinking of going inside
to get warm, but the tiny puppy was
obviously having such a good time that
she didn't want to spoil his enjoyment.

"You are cold, Robyn," Storm
noticed. "I will make you warm."

A familiar warm tickling sensation
ran down Robyn's backbone as tiny gold
sparks bloomed deep within his fluffy
white coat. Instantly, she felt a thick layer
of fur lining her jeans, her jacket, and
even her gloves, and she was as warm as
toast.

"Thanks, Storm, that's much better.
Oh, look!" Robyn breathed in wonder
as a shifting curtain of glowing greenish
lights appeared and began rippling
across the clear winter sky. "Those must

be the Northern Lights. Aren't they amazing?"

"They are like the lights of my homeland. We often see them in the sky," Storm woofed softly, sounding a little sad.

Robyn wondered what Storm's home world was like. Perhaps it was a land of ice and snow, too. It must be a strange and wild place, where the great magical wolves that lived there fought over their lands. She felt a pang as she thought that Storm might be homesick and thinking of his wounded mother and the scattered Moon-claw pack.

Bowing her head, Robyn kissed the top of Storm's silky little head and held him close.

"Robyn? Is it really you?" called a voice.

Robyn almost jumped out of her skin. She spun round to see the slim, dark-haired girl from the knitwear shop standing there with a broad smile on her face.

"Krista!" she said delightedly. "What are you doing here?"

Krista smiled. She wore a red parka with a fur-trimmed hood. "I am on my way back home, with my uncle and aunt. I did not realize that you were on a cruise around the coast. We use the coastal steamers, like *Sea Princess*, as local ferries to get around."

Robyn remembered seeing that *Sea Princess* had a ferry and car deck. "Where do you live? Is it very far

away?" she asked, hoping that there might be time for her and Storm to get to know Krista better.

Krista told her. "We will reach the port in two days, on Christmas Eve. My village is a short distance inland. I live there with my mother and father, my brothers and sisters, my aunts, uncles and cousins, and all the rest of my family.

I will be very glad to see them again."

"You live with *all* of your family?"
Robyn asked curiously. She did get a bit
lonely with her dad away a lot of the
time, but Robyn wasn't sure she'd want to
live with a whole lot of other people.
"Do you travel around a lot after your
reindeer herds? Sorry. I didn't mean to
sound nosy. I'm just interested," she said,
blushing as she realized that she seemed to
be asking lots of questions.

Krista laughed. "That is all right. At
this time of the year, we live in houses,
but others, like my grandmother and
grandfather prefer to live in a *lavvo*—that's
a traditional tent," she explained. "Lots
of other Sami families live in the
village, too. We make things to sell,
until the season for calves to be born,

and then everyone helps out with the hard work."

"Cool," Robyn said, fascinated. Krista's life was completely different to her own. It sounded so busy and exciting.

Krista smiled at her enthusiasm and her slanted dark eyes twinkled. "Would you and your parents like to visit my village and meet my family?"

"Would I? I'd love it!" Robyn said at once. "But I'll have to ask my mom and dad if it's okay. They're in the main lounge. Why don't you come with me, and then you can meet them?"

Krista nodded. "I would like that. I will go and get Uncle Nikolai and Aunt Jorun. They would like to meet your parents, too."

As Robyn went belowdecks with

Krista, she whispered to Storm, "Isn't it great that we've bumped into Krista again?"

Storm's little face lit up, and he woofed in agreement.

Robyn woke the following morning, feeling full of excitement. Storm was curled in the crook of her arm. As she stirred, he opened one eye and then tucked his nose back between his paws.

"Come on, sleepyhead!" Robyn teased, gently tickling his furry little

sides. "We're meeting Krista for breakfast."

Storm stuck out all four fluffy white legs and had a big stretch before jumping to the floor.

Robyn threw back the quilt and got dressed quickly. Her parents were showered and ready, and they all went to the restaurant together. Robyn spotted Krista at a table the moment she and Storm walked in. She waved to her as she helped herself from the usual display of delicious food.

"Hi," Robyn said as she went and sat next to Krista.

"Hello, Robyn. Did you sleep well?"

"Yes, thanks. Oops," Robyn said, as she felt Storm scrabbling up on to her lap. She pretended to drop her fork and just managed to stop him from slipping off again.

The adults joined them with their plates of food. Mr. Parsons and Uncle Nikolai began chatting about soccer. Robyn's mom and Aunt Jorun talked about knitting, having discovered that they shared a passion for crafts the previous night.

"They all seem to be getting along very well, don't they?" Robyn commented to Krista.

"Yes, they do," Krista said. "I am very pleased that your parents have accepted my invitation to visit our village."

"Me too. I can't wait," Robyn said eagerly.

"I'm glad you said that," Krista replied, her eyes glinting mysteriously. "I have told my cousin Morten that you are coming to visit. He is arranging a surprise for you."

Robyn smiled, wondering what it could be.

Chapter
EIGHT

Later that day, Robyn and Storm were walking past some fishing boats frozen into the ice on a village wharf, on their way to meet up with her mom and dad who were in the supermarket. Robyn couldn't stop thinking about what Krista's surprise might be. She smiled down at Storm happily—this was turning out to be one of her best Christmases ever.

Suddenly, Robyn heard some furious
snapping and growling. It was coming
from a car parked outside a supermarket.
In the back were two large dogs, who
were scrabbling at the window.

Storm whimpered in terror and
cowered against Robyn's legs. She could

feel him trembling from head to foot through her warm boots.

"Shadow knows where I am. He has sent those dogs to attack me," Storm whined.

Robyn tensed as she saw the streetlights gleaming on the dogs' pale eyes and extra large teeth. How was she going to save her little friend? She was just about to pick Storm up and run away as fast as her legs would carry her when a man came out of the supermarket and got into the car. The fierce growling and barking eventually faded as the car pulled away.

"Those horrible dogs have gone now. You're safe with me," Robyn said. She picked Storm up and hurried onto a narrow side street.

The tiny puppy pressed himself against her and looked up at her with fearful eyes. "For now, perhaps, but Shadow will use his magic on other dogs we meet. If any of them find me, I may have to leave quickly, without saying good-bye."

Robyn couldn't bear to think of losing Storm so suddenly. "Maybe if we hide you really well, Shadow will give up looking for you and then you can stay with me forever. I'll take you home with me when the cruise ends. You'll love it there."

Storm reached up and touched her face with one fluffy, white front paw.

"That is not possible. One day, I must return to my homeland to lead the Moon-claw pack. Do you understand that, Robyn?" he barked, his little face serious.

Robyn swallowed hard, but she forced herself to nod as she went back toward the supermarket. She didn't want to think about anything, except enjoying every single moment of her Christmas vacation with Storm.

Christmas Eve finally arrived, and Robyn and Storm stood beside Krista as *Sea Princess* steamed into the harbor with her horn blaring. The grayish winter light hung over the small town, which banked steeply up the hillside behind the harbor.

The ship was only staying for a few hours, as the Christmas festivities would soon begin on board.

"Will it take long to get to where you live?" Mrs. Parsons asked Krista.

"Not long at all." Krista looked at Robyn and her lips curved in another of her mysterious smiles.

Robyn was puzzled. What could Krista be planning?

Ten minutes later, when she and Storm were getting off the ship, Robyn gave a cry of delight. A beautiful wooden sleigh, pulled by two reindeer in brightly colored harnesses with woolen tassels stood waiting.

"Wow! This is fantastic," Robyn enthused.

"What a wonderful surprise," her dad said.

Krista smiled. "I thought you would like it. This is Morten, my cousin," she said, introducing the tall young sleigh driver.

"Pleased to meet you," Robyn said, smiling.

Robyn's mom and dad greeted him, and then Morten helped them climb aboard the sleigh, before helping to load the supplies.

Robyn settled Storm on her lap and they nestled beneath the warmth of the thick furs. Krista sat next to her. Once everyone was settled, Morten twitched the reins and the reindeer sped off across the snow in a jingle of sleigh bells.

"This reminds me of that "Winter Wonderland" song!" Robyn's dad said. "In the lane, snow is glistening. Can't you hear, logs are blistering . . . ," he

began, singing all the wrong words.

Robyn saw her mom give him one of her looks and poke him in the ribs.

Robyn stifled a giggle as her dad fell silent. Krista glanced at her mom, and they both burst out laughing.

Storm sat upright on Robyn's lap, looking around at the thick blanket of white snow. More flakes began to fall, dancing in the glow of the sleigh lanterns.

Soon lights were visible in the gloom ahead. Robyn saw buildings with grass poking up through the snow on their roofs. Tall, cone-shaped tents were dotted around. She could smell wood smoke on the frosty air.

As Morten brought the sleigh to a halt, people hurried out to welcome back Krista and her aunt and uncle. Robyn smiled and shook hands as she was introduced to Krista's parents, her brothers and sisters, and countless aunts and uncles and cousins. She knew she'd never remember all of their names.

"My grandparents would like to welcome you to their *lavvo*," Krista explained. Robyn, Storm, and the adults were shown inside one of the tents.

Colorful wall hangings and a crackling log fire inside the *lavvo* made it very warm and cozy. Delicious smells came from a metal cooking pot hanging over the flames. Robyn sat down close to the fire, and Storm came and curled up beside her.

Krista's grandparents made them very welcome with food and hot drinks. Afterward, a woman entertained them with traditional chanting and storytelling, while playing on a skin drum covered with drawings.

"We call this *joik*," Krista told Robyn. "Storytelling is an old tradition of my people."

Storm sat up and pricked his ears, enjoying the entertainment. "I like this place," he woofed.

Robyn reached down to pat him, to show that she did too. But she didn't dare risk whispering to him with all the people around.

Krista showed Robyn around her house, too. It was similar to the houses back home, with a modern TV and a computer, but there was a large wooden hut and a wooden pen for reindeer attached to the side of it. Krista's mom made fabulous jewelry with silver wire.

Time passed all too quickly and soon they had to return to *Sea Princess*.

There were many good-byes and hugs all around. Morten drove the reindeer sleigh back to the harbor, and Krista insisted on coming along with Robyn to keep her company.

As the sleigh drew to a halt at the harbor beside the huge bulk of *Sea Princess*, Krista slipped something into Robyn's hand.

"I made this. It is for you," she said.

Robyn looked down to see that it was a tiny reindeer-horn carving of an arctic wolf. The tiny wolf looked just like Storm as his real self. It even had chips of some glittery dark-blue material for eyes.

"Oh, it's beautiful. Thank you," she said warmly, giving Krista a hug.

"I am glad that you like it," Krista said, her tilted dark eyes moist.

"I love it so much," Robyn said with a catch in her voice. "Good-bye, Krista. And thanks for letting me meet your family. I had the best time ever. I'll send you an e-mail when I get back home."

Krista's face brightened. "Oh yes, please do. And maybe we can talk online. It will be wonderful to keep in touch with each other."

"Definitely!" Robyn promised. She wished this Christmas could last forever.

Chapter
NINE

Robyn stood on board *Sea Princess*
with Storm in her arms. They were
looking down at the harbor, where
Morten was turning the sleigh around.
The reindeer and Krista, huddled in
the sleigh among the furs, looked tiny
now.

Krista waved one small mitten as
the reindeer plunged forward and the

sleigh moved smoothly away on wooden
runners.

"Good-bye. Safe journey!" she called.

"Good-bye!" Robyn cried, waving.

She and Storm waited until they could
no longer hear the sound of sleigh bells
before going inside the ship.

Robyn's mom walked beside her.
"Well, that was wonderful, wasn't it?

Krista's family was so hospitable. You
must get me their address. I'd love to
send them something from home when
we get back."

Robyn thought that was a great idea.

"Well, shall we go and see if
anything's happening in the lounge yet?
I feel like singing a few carols," her dad
said.

"Sounds great. I'll just be a minute. I
want to get something from the cabin,"
Robyn replied.

She was going to grab the gloves
and wallet, which were hidden at the
end of her bunk. She wanted to wrap
them and then sneak them under the
enormous Christmas tree, so her mom
and dad would be able to open them
later.

Storm padded beside Robyn at her heel as she went belowdecks. They had just stepped into the corridor leading to their cabin when Storm gave a yelp of terror and shot forward.

"What's wrong?" Robyn said, frowning.

Storm stood beside the cabin door, pawing frantically at it. She could see that he was trembling from head to foot.

Suddenly, Robyn heard fierce growling. Whipping around, she saw the shadows of two large dogs coming down the stairwell on the wall behind her.

Robyn's heart missed a beat. Shadow must have found Storm when they were on land and sent his dogs onto the ship after him! The puppy was in terrible danger.

Robyn didn't think twice. She
hurtled down the corridor and unlocked
the cabin door with shaking fingers. She
and Storm dashed inside, just as a fierce
snapping and growling sounded right
behind them.

"Oh!" Robyn shielded her eyes with
her hand as a dazzling flash lit up the
entire cabin.

Storm stood before her, a tiny fluffy
white puppy no longer, but a majestic
young silver-gray wolf. Hundreds of tiny
diamond-bright lights glowed from his
thick neck-ruff. Beside him stood a larger
wolf with a gentle expression and large
golden eyes.

And then Robyn knew that Storm
was leaving for real.

She went forward and threw her arms

around the wolf's neck. "I'll never forget
you, Storm," she said.

Storm allowed her to hug him for
a moment and then gently pulled away.
"You have been a good friend, Robyn.
Be of strong heart," he rumbled in a deep,
velvety growl.

Robyn nodded, unable to speak as
she felt a tear run down her cheek. She
remembered that she hadn't been able

to get Storm a Christmas present. It
seemed wrong not to give him something.

She had a sudden thought. "Please,
wait!" Reaching into her pocket, she took
out Krista's gift. She held it out to Storm.
"This is for you. To remind you that, one
day, you'll be a great leader of the Moon-
claw pack," she murmured.

Storm reached out and closed his huge
paw over the tiny carved wolf. "Thank
you, Robyn. You are very kind."

There was a final burst of intense gold
light and a great shower of gold sparks
exploded silently into the air and drifted
harmlessly down around her. Storm and
his mother faded and were gone.

The fierce growling outside the cabin
stopped and silence fell.

Robyn felt a deep ache. She would

never forget Storm, but she would always have her memories of the incredible Christmas vacation she had shared with the magic puppy.

The cabin door opened and her dad stood there. "Oh, there you are, honey. Are you coming up to the lounge? There's a carol service on, and afterward Santa Claus is going to hand out presents."

Robyn quickly wiped away a tear and smiled. "Just coming!"

A little reindeer needs a friend!

Magic Reindeer

A Christmas Wish

SUE BENTLEY

To our animal friends everywhere. We love you.

Magic Reindeer

A Christmas Wish

SUE BENTLEY

illustrated by Angela Swan

Prologue

"I'm coming, too!" Starshine cried, galloping toward the ice bridge after the White Crystal Reindeer Herd. As he lifted his head, his chocolate-brown eyes flashed with determination.

It would be a long journey through the night sky to deliver presents to children all over the world. But Starshine had been practicing by leaping high over the snow-covered trees and galloping among the stars. He knew he was ready to join the other reindeer.

Moonlight gleamed on the young reindeer's fluffy white coat and glowing gold antlers and hooves. The tiny gold snow globe he wore on a chain around his neck tinkled softly.

"Yay!" Starshine cried, and, with a twitch of his short tail, he soared up into the night sky.

Just ahead of him galloped his older brothers, Moonfleet and Dazzler. The herd stretched into a single line as they sped ever higher, leaving a silvery trail of hoofprints behind them in the air.

Starshine panted a little as he strained to keep up.

Suddenly there was a bright flash

and an enormous reindeer with a wise expression appeared next to him. He had a thick golden neck ruff and magnificent spreading antlers.

"Father!"

Starshine puffed out his little chest. How proud of him the reindeer king must be.

"I know that you are eager to run with us, Starshine. But you are not yet ready for this task. Turn back now," the king said gently in a deep, soft voice.

"But I am strong and fast!" Starshine protested. "Please let me go with you!"

The king shook his head, his deep amber eyes gleaming with affection. "That is not possible, my son. We have a long way to go and many presents to deliver. I am afraid that you would hold us up."

"I won't," Starshine began. "I promise—"

"That is enough," the king said firmly. "Return to Ice Mountain Castle, Starshine. We will speak of this later."

The young reindeer bowed his head. "Yes, Father." He hung back a little as his father rejoined the herd. They disappeared into the night and their trail of shimmering silver hoofprints began to grow fainter.

Starshine glanced dejectedly over his shoulder. His icy home world was just visible far below him. Why did *he* have to return to their castle just because he was the youngest? It wasn't fair. Moonfleet and Dazzler had all the fun.

He'd prove to them all that he *could* keep up! On impulse, the young magic reindeer leaped forward again. His breath came fast as he galloped through the star-pricked blackness.

But where was the trail? He couldn't see a single glowing hoofprint. Starshine kicked at the air in panic; his legs felt so heavy.

"Help! I'm lost!" he bleated. But there was no one to hear him. The golden snow globe around his neck began to glow. There was a flash of dazzling bright light, and a starry mist of silver and gold surrounded him. Starshine snorted weakly as he felt the magic envelop him and float him gently downward . . .

Chapter ONE

"Marie Zaleski?" the class teacher called, looking up from the attendance book.

"Yes, sir!" Marie answered. She blushed as there was a ripple of laughter from the girls sitting at the desk opposite.

"You're supposed to say, 'Here, Mr. Carpenter,'" Shannon James said. "But he wouldn't understand you anyway!"

Shannon was the most popular girl in the class. She had shiny dark-brown hair and a pretty, heart-shaped face.

Marie went even redder. She had lived in Poland for most of her nine years. She spoke perfect English, but Shannon took every opportunity to tease her about her accent.

"I like the way Marie talks. It's different," said a boy's voice from the desk next to Shannon. It was Chris Robins, a lively boy with a playful expression who was always joking around.

Marie turned and darted a quick, shy look at him.

"Yeah, right!" Shannon crowed, grinning. "You would say that, Chris!"

There was another burst of laughter. As Chris joined in, Marie sank down in her seat. Maybe he'd only been pretending to stick up for her, so he could tease her even more. She shook her head slowly as she thought that she didn't understand these kids. They often said one thing and meant another.

"All right, class. Quiet down," Mr. Carpenter ordered, closing the attendance book. "Open your history textbooks, please. We'll continue reading about how the Victorians celebrated Christmas. After morning break, we'll start making classroom decorations."

"Mr. Carpenter?" Shannon put up her hand. "Is it true that this year's play is going to be a musical?"

"That's right. We'll be choosing people to play the lead roles tomorrow or the day after," the teacher explained.

"Great!" Shannon wiggled excitedly. "I'm going to be Mary, Baby Jesus's mother!" she said confidently.

Mr. Carpenter smiled. "Are you sure? That's a big part with some difficult songs."

"Shannon's got a really good voice!" Chris called out. "You just wait until you hear it!"

Shannon grinned smugly as there was a cheer from her classmates. Marie didn't know whether she should join in. She decided not to, in case she drew more attention to herself, and bent over her textbook instead.

On one page there was a picture of a Victorian family standing around a prettily decorated Christmas tree with colorful wrapped presents at its base. Outside the window, carolers stood in the snow. It looked like the perfect family Christmas. Marie sighed unhappily, wishing that *her* family could all be together for this first Christmas in America. But her dad had stayed behind in Poland because his sister was sick. Marie and her mom were staying with Gran and Gramps, and Dad was hoping to join them soon.

Marie glanced out of a nearby window where the playground was just visible through lashing rain. Everything was gray, damp, and miserable. The morning seemed to drag on forever. But she cheered up a little after the break when they started on the decorations.

Marie loved making things, and she was really good at it. After folding up some white paper, she carefully cut out shapes along the fold lines. When she opened the paper it turned into a pretty garland of lacy snowflakes.

As she dabbed on glue and sprinkled
on dustings of silver glitter, she thought of
Poland. It had been snowing when she and
her family left. Everything was gleaming
white. The air was crisp and so cold it made
your nose prickle to breathe. *This snowflake
garland reminds me of home*, she thought.

And then she remembered, with a pang,
that *this* was now her home.

Deep in thought, she didn't notice
Chris creeping up behind her with a
rubber-band stretched across his fingers like
a catapult.

"Hey! Marie!" he called. "That's a really
cool decoration!"

Taken by surprise, she whipped
around, just as he twanged the band at
her. It pinged her forehead, just above her
eyebrow.

"Ow!" she cried and, to her horror, felt tears stinging her eyes—even though it didn't actually hurt that much.

"Good shot, Chris!" Shannon crowed.

But Chris's face fell. "Sorry. It was a joke. I didn't mean—"

Marie didn't want to hear it. She'd had enough of these mean, unfriendly kids.

"Yes you did!" she cried, her temper rising. "Why don't you just leave me alone?" Jumping to her feet, she ran toward the door. "I . . . I need to go to the bathroom," she murmured to the surprised teacher as she hurtled past him.

She only meant to go and sit in the coatroom until she calmed down. But somehow her feet kept right on going, taking her outside and across the playground. She spotted the bleachers, which were out of sight of the classrooms, and dived behind them.

I hate it here! I wish we'd never come! she said to herself, wiping away tears with the back of her hand. It wasn't fair. Why couldn't her mom have found a new job in a children's hospital in Poland instead of here? Marie made a decision. She was going straight home to Gran and Gramps's house. And she was never coming back to this dumb school where everyone was too busy to bother with a new girl.

Maybe Mom will let me be homeschooled, she thought, as she prepared to make a dash for the school gate. She rocked forward on to her toes. *One! Two! Thr–*

Suddenly there was a bright flash of light, and a mist made up of millions of tiny gold and silver stars filled the air around her. Marie noticed glittery stars forming and twinkling on her skin.

"Oh!" She screwed up her eyes, trying to see through the strange shining mist.

As it cleared, Marie noticed a fluffy white reindeer with a softly glowing

coat and little golden antlers and hooves walking slowly toward her. Around its neck it wore something that looked like a tiny golden charm on a delicate chain.

It gave a scared little bleat. "Can you help me, please?"

Chapter
TWO

Marie's eyes widened as she stared at the cute little reindeer in astonishment. She had no idea what it was doing here behind the school bleachers, but she was pretty sure that reindeer couldn't talk.

"Hello, there," she said softly, thinking she must be imagining it all. "Where did you come from?"

The reindeer's sensitive white ears

flickered, and she saw that it had big chocolate-brown eyes. "I have just arrived here. I was following my herd when I became lost. What is this place?"

Marie did a double take. She felt like pinching herself to make sure she wasn't

dreaming. But the little reindeer was looking intently at her, as if expecting an answer.

"This is . . . um, Chiltern Park Elementary School," she told him.

"I do not know this place. I think I am a long way from home," the reindeer said thoughtfully. "My name is Starshine of the White Crystal Herd. What is yours?"

"I—I'm Marie. Marie Zaleski," she stuttered, still not quite believing that she was actually talking to a reindeer. This was like something out of the Polish folktales her dad told her.

Starshine bent his knees and dipped his head in a formal bow. His golden antlers left a trail of sparkling bright light, which swiftly faded as he straightened up. "I am honored to meet you, Marie," he snorted softly.

"Um . . . likewise," Marie said, dipping her chin politely. "Where did you come from? And how come you can talk, if . . . um, you don't mind me asking," she added, keeping very still so that she wouldn't frighten this amazing creature away.

Starshine flicked his little moplike white tail. "All the White Crystal Reindeer can talk. We live in Ice Mountain Castle in a faraway world, with my father and mother, who are our king and queen. I have two older brothers, Dazzler and Moonfleet. I am the youngest reindeer in the herd"—Starshine lifted his head proudly—"but I am ready to do my duty and deliver presents all over the world to make people happy."

Marie was fascinated. She was still

trying to take this all in. The little reindeer's world sounded so strange and magical. Something he said puzzled her, though. "You deliver things all over the world? But how . . . ?"

"My magic snow globe helps me. I will show you," Starshine snuffled, backing away.

Marie felt a warm prickling sensation flowing down the back of her neck as what she had thought to be a tiny golden charm on the chain around his neck began to glow and get bigger. An image appeared inside the clear crystal globe.

Marie leaned forward curiously. She saw an amazing icy world of endless snow-covered peaks, blue glaciers, and frozen seas. Topping a massive cliff of ice was a tall building with spires and turrets.

It looked like a sparkling cathedral made of glass.

She saw Starshine—a tiny white shape standing on an icy platform. He glowed so brightly with golden light that Marie had to shade her eyes to look at him. Sparks glinted in his fur and his chocolate-brown eyes twinkled with gold. Around him were lots of older reindeer, all with sparkling white coats, large golden antlers, and golden hooves.

As she watched, a line of reindeer appeared in the sky above the castle, leaving a trail of sparkling golden hoofprints behind them. They swept downward and landed beside Starshine.

Marie realized that she was watching events that must have already happened before Starshine came to her world.

"Wow!" she breathed in total wonderment. She had never seen anything so beautiful in her entire life. Starshine was cute and pretty with his fluffy white coat and dewy eyes, but in his own world— surrounded by that dazzling halo of golden light—he was a magnificent sight. "Is that really where you live with the White Crystal Herd?"

Starshine nodded, his brown eyes now shadowed by homesickness. "Yes. That is Ice Mountain Castle," he told her with a little catch in his voice. "I followed the others when they left on a trip, but Father told me to go home. I thought I was strong enough to keep up. But I grew tired and became lost. My magic snow globe brought me here." Starshine dipped his head and looked up at her with big sad

eyes. "I miss my family very much. Will
you help me find my way back to them?"

Marie's heart melted. She knew how
it felt to be lonely and miss someone you
loved who was far away. "Of course I'll
help you. What do I have to do?"

Starshine flicked his little white ears
and seemed to cheer up a bit. "We must
watch the night sky together for a trail of
sparkling hoofprints. It will be invisible to

most people in this world, but you will be able to see it if you are with me or very close to me."

"All right. We'll keep a lookout for it," Marie said. "Maybe Mom and Gran and Gramps could help us, too? I can't wait to tell them about you!"

Starshine lifted his head. "I am sorry, Marie. You can tell no one about me or what I have told you."

Marie felt disappointed that she couldn't confide in anyone. But then she thought about how awful today had already been, and she decided that it might be nice to have a special secret of her own. She felt proud that Starshine had chosen her to help him. At least now she had a real friend who understood exactly how she felt.

"You must promise me, Marie,"
Starshine insisted, blinking at her with his
intelligent eyes.

Marie nodded. She was determined to
do all she could to keep Starshine safe and
help him return to his magical ice world
and his family. As she was wondering
whether or not to leave for home now—
and take Starshine with her—a girl walked
behind the bleachers.

It was Shannon James.

"Mr. Carpenter sent me to find you.
I've been looking everywhere for you.
Why are you hiding out here?" she asked.

Marie panicked. Any minute now
Shannon was going to see the little magic
reindeer! Marie had to do something.
Spreading her arms wide, she did a funny
little sideways shuffle that hid him from

view. She hoped he'd get the message and quickly hide.

The other girl gaped at her in surprise. "What are you doing?"

Marie continued to skip about and wave her arms. "Dancing. I'm trying to . . . um, keep warm," she fibbed hastily. "I came out here for some fresh air. But I forgot my coat, and it's a bit cold." She swirled around in a circle and saw with surprise that Starshine hadn't moved. He was watching her, his mouth twitching with amusement.

"That is a very good dance," he snuffled.

Marie did a double take. What was going on? How come Starshine had just spoken in front of Shannon? And why didn't she seem to see him?

The other girl's lip curled. "You can stop that stupid dancing. Do you think I don't know what you're up to? You were going to sneak home, weren't you?"

Feeling a little silly now, Marie came to a sudden halt. "What do you care? It's not as if anyone's going to miss me— especially you."

"I knew it!" Shannon crowed triumphantly. "Let's see what Mr. Carpenter has to say when I tell him!"

"Wait!" Marie called, but the other girl was already heading back toward the classrooms. "Oh, great," she groaned.

"Is something wrong, Marie?" Starshine snorted in concern.

Marie nodded. "I hate this school. I was just about to leave when you appeared. But it's too late now . . ." Starshine listened closely, his velvety nose twitching as she explained that no one seemed to want to be her friend.

"I suppose I'd better go back into class, or there'll be a huge mess," Marie sighed. "How come Shannon didn't notice you?"

"I used my magic. Only you can see and hear me," Starshine told her.

"You can make yourself invisible? Wow! You'll definitely be safe behind the bleachers then. So I'll see you after school?"

Starshine put his head on one side. "No, Marie. I will not be here."

Marie felt a stir of panic at the thought that he was going to leave. She'd hardly got used to the idea of having him as a friend.

"But where are you going?" she asked, worried. She knew it. The first real friend she'd made and he was leaving already!

Chapter THREE

The reindeer pawed the ground excitedly with one front hoof. "I am coming into school with you!" he exclaimed in a soft rumbling bellow.

"Really?" Marie felt a big grin spread across her face. This was awesome. She was finally going to have a friend in her class! But who'd have thought it would be a magic reindeer?

"How's that going to work?" she wondered aloud. "You're too big to hide under my desk or sit on my lap. Even if you're invisible, people could still bump into you and you could get hurt."

Starshine's dewy eyes twinkled mischievously.

Marie felt another warm prickling sensation at the back of her neck as the tiny golden snow globe began to glow brightly again. There was a flash of silver and gold starry light, and the reindeer disappeared. In his place stood a tiny stuffed version of himself.

"Wow! That's amazing," Marie said breathlessly, reaching down to pick up the toy.

Starshine just fit into her cupped hands. He had the tiniest, sweetest little

hooves, cute ears and antlers, and beautiful
brown eyes. As she stroked his petal-soft
white fur, she thought that she'd never
felt anything so gorgeous and velvety.
Starshine snorted with pleasure.

He was gorgeous as a young magic
reindeer and magnificent as a glowing
golden prince in his own icy world, but
as a fluffy little toy, Starshine was totally
adorable!

"Now you can come everywhere with me," Marie said enthusiastically. "You don't even have to worry about people seeing you. And you can sleep in my bedroom at home!"

"That sounds like fun. Thank you, Marie," Starshine said in a tiny voice that matched his new size.

As Marie went back into school, her heart felt lighter than it had in ages. Even the prospect of facing Shannon and Mr. Carpenter didn't seem that scary. With Starshine tucked inside her school sweater, she already felt braver and a little less lonely.

No one said anything as Marie came back into the classroom and made her way to her seat. She felt relieved. Shannon obviously hadn't carried out her threat

about telling Mr. Carpenter that she was
going to leave school in the middle of
the day.

Marie glanced at the other girl as she
passed her, about to say thanks for not
tattling. But then she noticed her desk.
It was a complete mess, with paints and
paper and other art stuff all scattered
around.

The glittery paper snowflake garland

she'd made earlier was in a crumpled pile on her chair. Marie went to pick it up, but it was stuck. Someone had obviously thought it would be funny to glue it to her seat.

Marie had a decent idea who that "someone" was.

Shannon had a knowing grin on her face. She looked as if she was trying hard not to burst out laughing. "Problem?" she asked Marie innocently.

Marie didn't answer. Sighing, she placed Starshine on the empty seat next to her and began clearing up the mess. The desk was soon back to normal, but her chair was a different matter. She could only tear off jagged bits of the paper snowflake. "I was really happy with that decoration. It's ruined now," she murmured sadly.

"Do not worry, Marie. I will help you!" Starshine said with an eager little snort.

Marie looked at him curiously. "But how? What if someone sees you moving?" she whispered.

"To everyone but you, I appear to be an ordinary stuffed toy."

"Oh, I get it. You're using your magic again! That's so cool . . ." Marie only just stopped herself from gasping aloud as she felt a familiar prickling sensation and the snow globe around Starshine's neck began glowing brightly.

Whoosh! A cloud of sparkling mist, made up of the tiniest gold and silver stars imaginable, swirled around her chair.

Crackle! The snowflake garland pulled

free, did a quick shimmy in midair, and draped itself across her desk.

"It's all in one piece again! That's amazing!" Marie exclaimed, and then hastily began to "cough" as Shannon looked at her in surprise.

Marie looked down at her desk, pretending to be busy in case the other girl started asking awkward questions. Shannon obviously couldn't see the cloud of magical mist drifting across the classroom.

"Whoa! Cool!" Chris suddenly burst out.

Marie turned around to see him holding two tubes of colored glitter that were spurting into the air like fireworks and showing no signs of stopping. Across the room, some cans of spray

snow made burping noises and squirted
in all directions. Everywhere piles of
decorations began to multiply, until the
desks and floor disappeared beneath a
thick layer of glittering snowflakes, paper
lanterns, and paper chains.

Delighted kids leaped about, kicking
up the snow and glitter, and throwing
armfuls of decorations at each other.

"I think you used too much magic!"
Marie whispered tactfully.

"But look how everyone is laughing and enjoying themselves! I have made everyone happy!" Starshine twirled his tiny tail, looking very pleased with his magical results.

"Mr. Carpenter isn't!" Marie warned. "Look!"

The teacher was wading through the fake snow, decorations, and heaps of red, blue, and silver glitter, which formed a knee-deep layer around him.

"Goodness me!" Mr. Carpenter gasped. "I'll have to tell the principal about this. We seem to have been sent some faulty art supplies."

"Do something, Starshine! Quick!" Marie hissed, seeing that things were quickly getting out of control.

The magic reindeer looked

disappointed, but his snow globe flashed again and the magical mist disappeared in a flash. The glitter, spray-snow fountains, and growing piles of decorations all instantly collapsed into shimmering dust and disappeared. Finally, the classroom was normal again.

"Phew!" Marie said, relieved.

Mr. Carpenter was scratching his head and looking puzzled. The teacher clapped his hands for silence. "All right, class. The fun's over. Settle down and get back to work, please."

"That was a lot of fun!" Chris said, appearing at Marie's side. He smiled broadly at her. "What happened?"

"Me? How should I know?" Marie said, shrugging as she bit back a grin.

Chris seemed friendlier all of a sudden.

She thought his smile looked genuine, but it was hard to tell.

"What are you asking *her* for? She doesn't know anything," Shannon said, sauntering over. She gave Marie a hard look and then gave Chris a dig in the side.

"All right. Keep your shirt on!" Chris said, but he grinned over his shoulder at

Marie as he moved away.

Shannon noticed and didn't look pleased.

What's she got against me anyway? Marie thought. To her surprise, she found that she wasn't quite as upset by the girl's meanness as usual. Having Starshine around made all the difference.

"My magic did not make everyone happy. Shannon was not very nice to you. I have done wrong. Perhaps I am not ready to be a proper White Crystal Reindeer," Starshine said, looking crestfallen.

"Yes, you are," Marie reassured him in a soft voice. "You meant well. You just went a bit overboard with your magic."

Starshine blinked at her. "What is 'overboard'?"

"It means . . . um, a bit too enthusiastic," Marie explained.

"I understand. I think that is what my father and older brothers would say, too," Starshine said sadly. His ears drooped and his chocolate-brown eyes lost a little of their twinkle.

Marie could see that he was missing his family. She made sure no one was looking, before drawing him into her lap. As she stroked him, her heart went out to her little friend.

"I know how you feel. I miss my dad like crazy. Maybe we can help each other not to feel so lonely?"

Starshine nodded and nuzzled her hand with his tiny velvet-soft muzzle.

Chapter
FOUR

"Hi, Gran! I'm home!" Marie called as she entered the hallway after walking home from school.

Marie hung up her coat and took Starshine out of her schoolbag.

"This is a good place to stay until I find my way home," he said, looking around.

Gran appeared in the kitchen doorway. She spotted the magic reindeer before

Marie had a chance to smuggle him upstairs. "Hello, sweetie! What have you got there?" she asked.

"N-nothing!" Marie said in a panic, before she remembered that Gran could only see Starshine as a tiny toy reindeer. "I mean . . . um, one of the kids in class gave it to me."

"Well, that's nice," Gran said, smiling warmly. "It's a very cute toy. What dainty little antlers and hooves! I'm glad you're starting to make friends." She went to fill the kettle.

Marie followed her into the kitchen. She wondered what Gran would have said if she knew that her *only* friend was a magic reindeer. But, of course, she would never tell anyone Starshine's secret.

Then her mom arrived home from

work, and they all drank hot chocolate
and ate cookies in the kitchen. Gran
was saying how she wished they'd had
a chance to decorate the house before
Marie and her mom came to stay. "It's so
scruffy-looking. It hasn't been done in a
long time."

"It's fine, Mom. Don't worry about it,"
Mrs. Zaleski said.

Marie had Starshine on her lap, and
she was carefully slipping him little bits of
cookie. She noticed that he had pricked up

his ears and was listening closely to Gran.

"The older lady is not happy with her house," the little reindeer snuffled thoughtfully.

"Mmm. A lot of grown-ups say stuff like that." Marie whispered, patting him. She was thinking about the cozy bed she would make for him in her room.

She tucked Starshine under her arm, drained her mug, and put it in the dishwasher. "I'm going to do my homework," she announced to Mom and Gran, before trudging upstairs. Marie's small bedroom overlooked the front yard and street. Beside the bed, there was just space for a wardrobe, a bookcase, and a chest of drawers. A dollhouse, which Gran had found at a tag sale, stood on top of the chest.

Starshine was on the bedside rug, watching as Marie fished around in the wardrobe for a shoe box.

"I thought you could sleep in this!" she said, folding up a wool scarf and putting it in the box. "And you can snuggle up with me at night."

Starshine immediately leaped into the box and lay down, folding his legs beneath him. He looked so cute that Marie couldn't help smiling.

"I like it here, but human houses are very warm," he panted, showing his little pink tongue.

Marie remembered that her new friend came from a world of ice and snow and wasn't used to central heating in houses. "Oh, sorry! You must be absolutely boiling. I'll open my window."

She did so, and a blast of cold air filled the small room. Starshine lifted his head and his nose twitched with pleasure as he snuffed it up. "That is much better. Thank you, Marie."

"No problem," Marie said, hiding a shiver as she reached for another sweater. She didn't mind wearing extra clothes to keep warm, if it meant Starshine was comfortable.

She had a sudden thought. "You must be really hungry. Those pieces of cookie won't have filled you up. I can hear Mom and Gran in the living room. I'll sneak back downstairs to the kitchen and see what I can find. Back in a minute!"

Starshine's chocolate-brown eyes lit up. "That is good. My tummy is rumbling."

Luckily the kitchen was empty. Marie opened the fridge and looked inside, and then realized that she wasn't sure what reindeer ate. They were vegetarians, weren't they? On impulse, she grabbed a carrot and a couple of sticks of celery and then reached into the fruit bowl for an apple on her way out.

Back upstairs, Starshine eyed the fruit and vegetables warily. Reaching out, he sniffed the carrot and then took a tiny nibble. He nodded slowly, looking surprised, and then sampled the apple and celery. "Delicious!" he snorted, his eyes sparkling as he chomped. "I like human food."

"What do you usually eat?" Marie asked him.

"Grass, moss, and small plants we find by scratching away the snow," he told her.

Marie thought hard. She supposed he could eat the grass on the school playing fields, but Gran's yard didn't have a lawn. What was he going to eat at night and weekends? Mom or Gran were going to

notice if she kept taking stuff from the
fridge to feed him.

"I know! There's a pet store on the
way to school. They've got a special offer
on bags of hay. I can buy a small bag
tomorrow and smuggle it home in my
schoolbag."

"What is hay?"

"Dried grass, I think," Marie said.
"It's what lots of animals eat, like . . . um,
horses and rabbits."

Starshine nodded, licking his chops.
"Hay sounds good."

Marie gently stroked his fluffy coat
and warm little antlers. Starshine nudged
her very softly and licked her fingers.
His breath smelled warm and spicy like
Christmas cookies. She felt a surge of
affection for the tiny reindeer.

Just then she heard the phone ring downstairs in the hall.

"That might be Dad!" she said excitedly. "He usually calls around this time. Let's go and see!"

Starshine nodded his head.

Tucking him under her arm, Marie raced down the stairs two at a time and grabbed the phone.

"Hello, *aniołku*," said her dad's voice.

"Hi, Dad!" She loved the way he always called her his "angel." "How are you? How is Aunt Jolenta?"

Mr. Zaleski told Marie that her aunt was doing quite well, but he still couldn't leave her yet. They chatted for a few minutes. Marie told him about school and how things were a little better, but she didn't mention Starshine. He told her he missed her and then asked if she'd put her mom on the phone.

"*Kocham cię*, Marie."

"I love you, too, Dad," she said with a lump in her throat. "Please come here soon." Her mom had come into the hall and was standing beside her. Marie turned and passed her the phone.

As she wandered into the living room where Gran was collecting her library books and putting them in a bag, Marie blinked away tears. Now that she had Starshine for a friend, she didn't mind so much that she still hadn't made any friends at school. If only Dad could be here, then everything would be perfect.

"Do you two want to come to the library with me?" Gran asked when Marie's mom had finished talking to her dad.

Mrs. Zaleski nodded. "I could do with a change of scene. What about you, Marie?"

"I think I'll stay here," Marie decided, plunking herself on the sofa. She really wanted to curl up with Starshine and watch some TV.

But he had other ideas. As soon as the

car pulled out of the driveway, Starshine leaped off the sofa.

The moment his tiny hooves touched the carpet, he instantly grew to his normal size. "I know a way to make Gran happy with her house!"

Marie felt a warm prickling sensation at the back of her neck as Starshine's golden snow globe shone with power, and a sparkling gold and silver starry mist appeared.

Something very strange was about to happen.

Chapter
FIVE

Marie watched in total astonishment
as the magical starry mist swirled around
the room.

Rumble! All the furniture disappeared
and the walls stretched upward into jagged
icy peaks and a white domed ceiling.
Crackle! Ice sculptures, tables and sofas
carved into the shapes of swans appeared.
Rustle! Mountains of gold pillows plopped

onto the sofas and a shining golden carpet unrolled across the floor.

"Oh!" Marie gasped, horrified.

"Do you like it? It is just like a room in Ice Mountain Castle," Starshine said proudly.

"It's . . . um . . ." She searched for the right word. "Different?" She didn't think this was what Gran had in mind.

Just then there was the sound of a car outside in the driveway. Marie rushed over to the window. "It's Gran and Mom! They must have forgotten something! Quick, Starshine, put everything back as it was!"

"But it is so beautiful. Are you sure?" he bleated, disappointed.

"Yes! We have to do it now!" Marie cried in a panic.

Time seemed to stand still. Once again Marie felt a prickling sensation as Starshine's snow globe instantly worked its magic. In a flash of bright gold and silver stars, everything in the room shrank in size and the golden carpet folded itself up around them. With a swishing sound it tightened like a drawstring. *Flash!* It disappeared, returning the icy room to normal.

Marie breathed a sigh of relief. It was only just in time. "Hi, Mom!" she said brightly, as Mrs. Zaleski peeked her head around the door.

"Hi, honey. Silly me! I forgot my purse—" Her mom broke off in surprise. "Wherever did that great big reindeer come from?"

"What reind—" Marie's eyes widened

as she realized that Starshine was still his
full size and must have forgotten to be
invisible. She whirled around to him. "Oh,
that reindeer. It's . . . um, a prop for the
class play," she improvised, giving Starshine
a pleading look. Luckily, he caught on
quickly and didn't blink or move a single
muscle.

"It's much lighter to carry than it looks," Marie went on. "I said I'd . . . um, bring it home to . . . to spruce up the gold paint on its antlers. I'm taking it back with me tomorrow. I forgot to tell you."

Her mom nodded. "Good for you! It's great that you're starting to get more involved in school." She grabbed her bag from the table and went back out. "See you later!"

Marie waited until she heard the front door bang and the car drive away. "Phew! That was *too* close!"

Starshine hung his head and looked up at her with huge, sad brown eyes. "My magic went wrong again," he snorted regretfully. "And you could have been in terrible trouble. I am a very bad reindeer."

Marie's heart melted. She put her arms

around his neck and pressed her face to his fluffy warmth. "You're a good reindeer. The best there ever was and I love having you for my friend!" she said firmly. "You only want to make people happy."

Starshine pricked his ears and nodded. "That is true. The purpose of a White Crystal Reindeer is to deliver gifts and bring happiness."

"And that's a really kind thing to do. But you're not used to how things work here yet. So maybe you could check with me first next time, before you do any magic?" she suggested tactfully.

As she stepped back, she saw that Starshine's face was aglow and every trace of unhappiness had faded from his eyes. "You are so clever, Marie. That is exactly what I will do!" he promised.

"All right, class! We'll be choosing the lead parts for the school musical this morning! It's called *A Christmas Wish*," Mr. Carpenter announced the following day in the school hall.

"Yay! I've been waiting for this!" Shannon bounced up and down in her seat so that her shiny brown hair waved back and forth.

The teacher smiled as he took his seat at the piano. "Okay then, Shannon. Let's see what you can do."

Shannon sang a song from a well-known musical. She had a pleasant voice, but it wasn't very strong, and she wobbled on some of the higher notes. When she finished, everyone clapped. As Shannon went back to her seat, she smirked at Marie. "The part of Mary's got my name on it," she said confidently.

Marie sat quietly as various boys and girls came forward and sang the same song. Some were really good, but others were awful. It didn't matter. They all got a round of applause.

"Are you going to sing?" Starshine asked from where he lay in Marie's lap as a tiny, fluffy reindeer toy.

"I . . . I'm not sure I want to dare," Marie whispered to him. "Everyone here would only tease me."

In Poland, Marie had been in the choir at the local church. She loved acting and singing and would really have liked to be involved in the class play. But she didn't think it was worth making the effort. Anyway, the best parts were bound to be snapped up quickly.

"I think you should. I could help you get a part," the magic reindeer said eagerly, his tiny tail twirling.

Marie saw that the golden snow globe around his neck was beginning to glow.

"Remember what we said about doing magic?" she reminded him quickly. "It's not always the answer."

Starshine nodded, and the snow globe

returned to normal. Everyone had now returned to their seats. The teacher stood up and moved away from the piano. "Right, if there's no one else—" he began.

But Starshine's comment had made Marie think. She found herself putting him aside and getting to her feet. "I'd like to try for a part, please."

"Marie? Of course you can!" Mr. Carpenter smiled encouragingly as she walked toward him. He sat down at the piano and placed his hands on the keys. "Do you know this song?" He waited for her to nod. "All right then. Ready when you are."

Marie took a deep breath. Her hands trembled with nerves as she opened her mouth to begin. But only a dry croak came out.

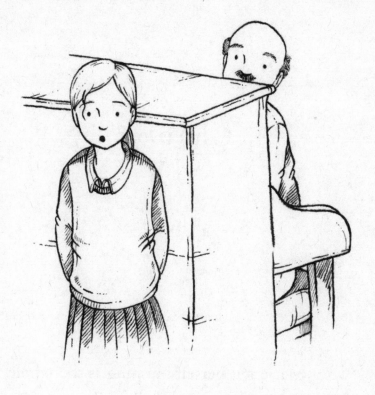

Chapter SIX

Marie felt herself blushing as the whole class erupted with laughter.

"There's not a part for a frog in the musical!" Shannon jeered.

The teacher held up his hands for silence. "Marie's just nervous. Let's give her a chance." He turned back to Marie. "Take a deep breath. There's no hurry. You tell me when," he said, smiling encouragingly.

Marie fought the urge to sink back into her seat. Mr. Carpenter was being really nice. She swallowed hard as she forced herself to relax. "Ready."

As Marie began to sing, she felt her earlier nerves pouring away. Her pure, sweet voice rang out into the hall. She reached the final high note, holding it easily until the song ended and the teacher lifted his hands from the keys.

There was a moment of stunned silence. Marie's heart sank. She knew she shouldn't have stood up to sing in front of everyone. They must have hated it!

But then someone started clapping slowly. Someone else joined in and then another person and then another . . . Soon wild applause rang out. Everyone was clapping like mad, except for Shannon.

She just sat there with her mouth open. For once, she didn't seem to know what to say.

"Way to go, Marie!" Chris yelled. "That was fantastic!" Marie looked across at him. He seemed to really mean it. She gave him a shy smile of thanks and he grinned back happily.

"Oh, shut up, Chris! She wasn't that good!" Shannon snapped.

But no one else agreed with her. Students that Marie had hardly spoken a word to came over to congratulate her. They wanted to know if she'd had singing lessons or been to theater school.

Marie shook her head. "I just love singing," she explained, overwhelmed by all the attention.

"Well, I think we've found our Mary!"
Mr. Carpenter said delightedly. "Marie
Zaleski will be playing the lead part.

Marie waited until she'd changed
out of her uniform after school before
telling her mom the good news. She'd left
Starshine munching hay in her bedroom.

"That's wonderful! My girl's going to
be a big star!" Mom gave her a huge hug.

"Mo-om!" Marie said, grinning. "It's

only a teeny part in the class play!"

"Well, I'm very proud of you," her mom said. "Come on. We're going out."

"Where are we going?"

"To the new Polish deli on Main Street. I wanted to get some groceries anyway. We'll celebrate with something nice to eat."

"I'll just get my bag," Marie said happily. She scooted upstairs to ask Starshine if he wanted to come, too. He'd finished his hay and jumped readily into her bag when she opened it for him.

It was only a short drive to the new delicatessen. Marie stood looking in the window while her mom put coins in the parking meter.

"Wow! Isn't this place amazing?" she said to Starshine.

The tiny magic reindeer nodded. He had reared up and looped his front legs over the edge of her bag so he could see the jewel-colored jars of jams, fruits, and pickles. A rich smell of coffee and fresh bread floated through the open door.

"Hi, Marie!" called a cheerful voice.

It was Chris, walking toward her with a broad smile on his face.

"Oh . . . um, hi," Marie answered.

"Congratulations again for getting the part in the play," he said, pausing.

"Thanks," Marie said, surprised and pleased. She remembered how he had seemed friendlier toward her in class lately, despite Shannon's influence.

"This is a nice deli," Chris said, looking in the window admiringly. "But I can't tell what some of the stuff is, unless there's a picture on the label. I bet you know, though, right?" he said, flashing her one of his playful grins.

Marie nodded, feeling a little self-conscious. But after a moment's hesitation, she read some of the labels aloud.

Chris listened closely. "That's a really cool language," he said when she'd finished. "Could you teach me some Polish?"

"Maybe," Marie said warily, waiting for the usual silly comment. But it never came. She wondered if Chris was actually being serious.

Mrs. Zaleski was finished at the car. She came over to them. "This is Chris. We're in the same class," Marie told her mom.

"Hi, Mrs. Zaleski," Chris said politely.

"Hi, Chris. It's nice to meet one of Marie's new friends. Would you like to join us for some cake?"

Marie looked at the ground, horrified. She couldn't believe her mom had just done that! Of course Chris would say no.

"Yeah—sounds great! Thanks, Mrs. Zaleski. That's okay with you, isn't it Marie?" Chris asked.

"Yes, of course." Marie felt a shy smile starting to spread across her face. "I hope they've got some honey cake. You'll love it. And there's this amazing milkshake . . ."

Later that day, as she lay on her bed reading a book of animal stories, Marie was still thinking about what a good time they'd all had. Starshine was beside her.

"Can you believe it? Mom really liked Chris. She even asked him to drop by our house over Christmas vacation. And he said he would!"

Starshine yawned and stretched out his little legs. "I like Chris, too."

Marie nodded slowly. Chris was much nicer outside school. For the first time, she wondered if she might have found another friend.

Chapter SEVEN

Rehearsals for *A Christmas Wish* took place over the next week. Marie and the other kids playing lead roles worked hard at learning their lines and practicing their songs. "I'm going to be onstage almost all the time. I hope I can remember everything," Marie whispered to Starshine. She reached out and stroked his soft white fur as he stood on her desk in his toy disguise.

His big chocolate-brown eyes sparkled at her. "You will be very good. I am looking forward to the play."

Marie smiled fondly at her magical friend. "I'm a bit nervous, but I'm looking forward to it, too!"

Shannon appeared beside her desk. "I can't believe I lost the best part in the play to a kid who brings stuffed toys to

school!" she said with disgust. "And now she's *talking* to it! How pathetic is that!"

"There's nothing wrong with liking toys." Marie put her arms around Starshine protectively.

"Yeah—if you're about four years old!" Shannon's lip curled as she stood there with her hands on her hips.

Before Marie could think of a reply, Chris called out. "I've got a teddy bear my mom bought me when I was a baby. So I guess that makes me pathetic, too, doesn't it?" he said, flashing Marie one of his playful grins.

"That's, um, different. Everyone knows teddy bears are cool," Shannon said, flustered. "Anyway, why are you taking her side? I thought family was supposed to stick together. You're *my* cousin—in case you've forgotten."

"I know that, but Marie's new in class. There's no need to pick on her," Chris said.

"I'm not!" Shannon snapped back sulkily. "What about *her*? She thinks she's just so cool for stealing my part!"

"Just leave it, Shannon," Chris said, rolling his eyes. He got up and sauntered across the room to a piece of cardboard shaped like a manger, which he was helping to paint.

"Yeah! You're right. She's not worth it!" Sticking her nose in the air, Shannon flounced after him.

Marie sat in stunned silence. Shannon and Chris were cousins? She hadn't realized they were related because they had different last names.

"How stupid am I for even thinking that Chris wanted to be my friend?" she whispered to Starshine. "He was just pretending to be interested in learning Polish so he and Shannon could tease me even more!"

Starshine's little ears drooped. "I did not think Chris was a mean person."

Marie didn't either, but she wasn't sure any more. Feeling tears well up in her eyes, she blinked them angrily. *Who needs friends in class anyway?* she fumed silently. She already had the best friend anyone could ever have in her magic little reindeer.

Marie slipped out into the yard with Starshine that evening. White frost sparkled on a bush near the patio and their breath steamed in the cold air.

With an eager little snuffle, Starshine turned back to his normal size, although he remained invisible. He reached out to nibble a couple of leaves from the bush.

"It is very strange to live in a world without snow," he commented, chewing.

"It was snowing when Mom and I left Poland," Marie said. "I hope we get some here. A white Christmas would be wonderful."

"I should be delivering presents all over the world with the other White Crystal Reindeer," Starshine said wistfully. He looked up into the night sky, which was dotted with millions of stars. Suddenly he stiffened.

Marie followed his gaze. There, spreading toward the horizon, was a trail of faintly glowing silver and gold hoofprints.

"My herd! They have been here!"
Starshine bleated excitedly.

She gasped. Did that mean that he
would be leaving to go after them?

"Are . . . are you going to try to catch
up with Moonfleet, Dazzler, and the
others?" she asked anxiously.

The young reindeer shook his head.
"No. The trail is cold and already fading.

But it proves they came this way. I will watch out for a fresh trail when they return. And then I may have to leave suddenly to follow them . . ."

"Oh." Marie felt a sharp pang as she thought of how lonely she would be without him. He was still her only friend. She realized that she would never be ready to lose him. "You . . . you could stay here with me if you wanted to," she said hopefully.

Starshine shook his head, his beautiful chocolate-brown eyes softening with affection. "That is not possible. I must return to my family in Ice Mountain Castle. I hope you understand, Marie."

Marie nodded sadly. She swallowed hard as she decided not to think about Starshine leaving. Instead, she promised

herself that she was going to enjoy every
single moment she had left with him.

Starshine bent his head and nuzzled her
sleeve with his sensitive nose; a cloud of
his warm sweet breath spread around her.

Marie put her arm around his neck and pressed her cheek to his fluffy warmth. "Let's go inside to my cozy bedroom and snuggle up together. It's freezing out here!" Starshine nodded, his golden antlers gleaming in the moonlight.

The next few days at school passed in a flurry of activity. Marie made sure she kept out of Shannon and Chris's way. But she caught Chris looking at her questioningly a few times. Once he started to come over to her, but she quickly walked away.

"I wish I could trust him," she confided to Starshine as they sat at her desk later. "But he's probably laughing about me behind my back with Shannon. They're always whispering together."

"I do not think Chris would do that," Starshine said. "Please do not be sad, Marie."

"Oh, I'm okay. I'm just a little annoyed, that's all," she admitted. "I'd started to like Chris."

"You need something to cheer you up!" Starshine decided, his eyes shining. "I have an idea! You were happy when you ate cake with your Mom and Chris in that store." His mouth curved as he showed his strong young teeth in an eager smile. Marie felt a familiar prickling at the back of her neck.

"Remember what we agreed about you being careful with your magic," she whispered warningly.

But it was too late. The snow globe around Starshine's neck began to glow and there was a bright flash, and a fountain of bright gold and silver sparks covered the empty chair beside Marie.

"Oh!" Marie blinked, rubbing her eyes as she noticed there was a big box full of delicious-looking cupcakes on the seat.

Starshine looked pleased with himself. "Now you can share these with everyone and have a good time!"

"Wow! These are gorgeous!" Marie felt relieved that, this time, Starshine didn't appear to have done anything too dramatic. She eyed the yummy cupcakes. They had frilly paper cases and pink, yellow, or white icing with glittery rainbow-colored sprinkles.

She picked up the box and took it over to the teacher. "I brought these for everyone to share. Would you like a cupcake, Mr. Roberts?"

The teacher's face lit up. "That's extremely kind of you, Marie. They look delicious." He took a bite. "Mmm, interesting flavor. Lemon and . . . is that sausage-flavor icing? Did you make them yourself?"

"Um . . . yes," Marie lied quickly,

hiding her surprise at the oddly flavored cupcake. She hurried across the classroom and offered the cupcakes to a group of kids who were painting scenery.

As kids helped themselves and began eating there was a ripple of excitement. "Cool! Mine's banana with ketchup-flavor icing!"

"Try this one! It's cucumber with chocolate!"

Marie smiled. As usual, Starshine had meant well, but in his enthusiasm he'd managed to mess up his magic! Luckily, everyone was having great fun sampling the weird flavors.

By the time Marie worked her way around to Chris and Shannon there were only three cupcakes left. Two ordinary-size ones, and a really large luscious one with

extra rainbow sprinkles. Marie frowned.
She was sure that the extra-big cupcake
hadn't been there earlier.

Glancing across at Starshine, she
noticed that he wore a mischievous
expression. *What's he up to now?* she
wondered.

"Thanks for bringing these in," Chris
said, smiling at Marie. "I hope they're as

good as that honey cake we had the other day with your mom."

"What honey cake?" Shannon said suspiciously, shoving past him to take the larger cupcake.

Shannon gave Marie a triumphant look as she took a huge bite. Suddenly her eyes bulged and she turned a sickly color. Diving across the classroom, she picked up the trashcan and practically stuck her head into it. "Yuck!" she spluttered, spraying cupcake crumbs everywhere. "Cough medicine with sardine-flavor icing!"

Chris burst out laughing. "Shame! Mine's strawberry with orange icing! Serves you right for being greedy! Great cupcakes, Marie."

As Marie returned Chris's smile, she started to feel bad about avoiding him.

He obviously hadn't told Shannon about the Polish deli. Maybe he didn't want his cousin to make mean comments or tease Marie about it. Marie wondered if she'd misjudged him and whether they might still be friends after all.

Chapter EIGHT

"Why does my magic keep going wrong?" Starshine asked mournfully when Marie finished giggling about the unusual flavor combinations of yesterday's cupcakes.

It was Saturday morning, and the two of them were snuggled up under the comforter.

"Well, maybe you still need to think a

little bit more before you do something," she suggested, stroking his tiny soft ears. "Dad always tells me that." She felt a flicker of sadness at the thought of her dad and wished he could be here to watch her in the class play.

Starshine sighed, nodding. "My father always says this, too. It is hard to do this when I just want to make everyone happy."

"I know. I suppose it's something you'll get better at with practice," Marie said soothingly. "Anyway, it didn't matter about your magic going wrong in class. Everyone had the best time—except for Shannon," she remembered with a chuckle. "That extra-big cupcake was genius!"

Starshine still looked subdued. He

twisted his head around and began glumly grooming his fluffy fur.

"You need cheering up!" Marie decided. She leaped out of bed and quickly dressed. "Come on!"

"Where are we going?"

"To the shopping mall. There's a Christmas fair going on! Let's go and see if Mom will take us."

Her toy-size friend leaped up eagerly, his tiny tail twirling, and they went downstairs together.

"What a good idea," Mrs. Zaleski said, when Marie asked her. "Maybe Gran and Gramps would like to come, too." After breakfast, everyone piled into the car and headed for the mall. Her mom parked in the parking garage and then they all piled in to the elevator.

"Here we go!" Gramps pressed a shiny button that said SHOPPING.

The sound of Christmas carols filled the air as the elevator doors opened. Marie and Starshine walked toward an open area that was surrounded with stores. It had been transformed into a winter wonderland.

Silver icicles and waterfalls of lights hung from every surface. Dozens of silver stars covered the ceiling and there was a giant Christmas tree sprayed with fake snow and glimmering with decorations. There was a big Christmas market, too.

Starshine peered out from the safety of Marie's bag with eyes as big as saucers. "This is wonderful!" he said happily. "It reminds me of Ice Mountain Castle."

"I'm glad you like it," Marie said,

pleased that her idea to cheer him up
appeared to be working. He seemed
happier already.

Mom, Gran, and Gramps wandered
around looking at the stalls that were piled
with cakes, cookies, and all kinds of treats.
There were wreaths, paper hats, and cans
of silly string, as well as dozens of different
decorations for sale.

Starshine's nose twitched at the smell
of roasting chestnuts. Marie bought some

and fed him tiny bits when no one was watching.

"Ho! Ho! Ho!"

With a jingle of sleigh bells, a white-bearded Santa in red robes trimmed with white fur appeared at the edge of the crowd. His gleaming sleigh was piled high with gifts and pulled by two real adult reindeer with spreading antlers.

Kids crowded close as Santa began giving out gifts, and Starshine spotted the two reindeer. He almost fell out of Marie's shoulder bag with excitement—his ears swiveled all over the place and his fluffy fur stood on end.

"Moonfleet! Dazzler! What are you doing here in disguise?" he brayed in delight.

Before Marie realized what was

happening, Starshine's snow globe glowed brightly and there was a flash of gold and silver sparks visible only to Marie as Starshine leaped high in the air. When they cleared, she saw that the magic reindeer stood there at his normal size.

A group of small children cheered and clapped. Luckily, everyone seemed to think that Starshine was part of the display.

"Wow! What a cute little white reindeer," one of them piped up.

"Look at his long lashes and pretty brown eyes," said a little girl.

As Starshine looked more closely at the two reindeer he seemed to realize his mistake. His head drooped. They were not his older brothers at all—they were just normal reindeer from this world.

Children were gathering excitedly

around Starshine. "Have you got presents for us, too?" a little boy asked.

Starshine turned around and around in circles. He looked confused by all the attention. But a pleased smile spread across his face as the crowd of kids pressed closer, patting him and stroking his soft white fur.

"Shall I use magic to make presents for them all?" he asked, looking uncertainly at Marie.

"No! Don't! It'll be total chaos!" she warned. Starshine was in danger of giving himself away at any moment.

Santa had noticed the commotion. "Oh! What's that white reindeer doing here?"

"Uh-oh!" Marie said under her breath, sensing trouble.

Santa walked toward Marie. His cheeks glowed an angry color that matched his red suit. "This is my spot. Have you got a license? Someone call security!" he shouted.

"Starshine! Make yourself tiny again," Marie whispered in a panic. "We need to get out of here . . . now!"

She felt a familiar prickling sensation at the back of her neck as the snow globe glowed again and Starshine seemed to disappear in the final flurry of gold and silver stars.

While Santa was still looking around for security, Marie bent down and swiftly picked up the toy reindeer before anyone stepped on him. Luckily, everyone else was looking at the shouting Santa and not at Starshine. She tucked him safely in her bag and began weaving through the crowd to where she could see her mom and grandparents.

"Oh there you are, sweetie," Mrs. Zaleski said. "Come on. We're about to have some hot chocolate and gingerbread."

"Great idea!" Marie said, breathless with relief.

She slipped one hand inside her bag and stroked Starshine, who rubbed his cheek against her hand and snuffled the tips of her fingers as a way of saying thank you.

A secret smile curved Marie's lips. Life was certainly never dull with Starshine around!

Chapter NINE

The morning of the class play dawned clear and cold. It was the day before Christmas Eve. The scenery was in place. The stage looked wonderful. Everything was ready.

Marie peeked out from behind the curtains at the packed school hall. She could see Mom, Gran, and Gramps in the audience. Her tummy cramped with nerves, and her fingers trembled as she smoothed her long blue costume and adjusted her headdress.

"Places everyone, please," Mr. Carpenter said.

Marie held her breath as the curtain began to rise.

Mr. Carpenter began playing the intro to the first song. Marie froze and she felt

sick. Could she really do this?

But she took a deep breath, stepped forward, and came in right on cue. Her voice wavered a bit, but she kept singing. Marie glanced into the wings. She saw Chris dressed as a shepherd in a tunic and a headdress made from a checked dish towel. Shannon stood next to him in an angel costume. Chris smiled and gave Marie a thumbs-up sign.

Then he nudged his cousin and— wonder of wonders—Shannon frowned, but did the same!

Marie smiled at them both gratefully. Her nerves had totally disappeared, and her voice swelled out strongly until it filled the hall with sweet, clear notes.

After that, the time seemed to fly. Everyone remembered their lines, and it all went well. Shannon sang her song and then passed Marie on the way to the wings.

On impulse Marie mouthed *good job* at her. Shannon blinked in surprise.

Suddenly the play was at an end. The audience clapped and cheered. Marie and the other players returned for not one but *three* curtain calls.

"They loved it!" Marie whispered delightedly to Starshine as she changed out of her costume.

Starshine beamed all over his face. His little golden antlers were glowing softly. "It was wonderful," he said breathlessly. "Everyone is so happy."

"You were pretty good," Shannon said at Marie's side.

"Thanks. So were you," Marie said.

"Look. Chris says you're okay, so maybe
we should try to get along," Shannon
murmured, staring at the ground. "I don't
mean best friends or anything, though!"

Marie nodded, shocked into silence.

As the other girl walked away, she
looked at Starshine in amazement. "Can
you believe it? Shannon James just spoke
to me nicely—for the first time! You
didn't have anything to do with it, did
you?" she asked suspiciously.

The magic reindeer shook his head.
"Certainly not! I have learned my lesson.
Now I think first before I do any magic!"

Marie felt a surge of pride for her
friend. "That's fantastic. Good job,
Starshine!" she praised. "The other White
Crystal Reindeer will be proud of you."

Starshine's chocolate-brown eyes

glowed with happiness.

After she'd changed, Marie met Mom, Gran, and Gramps in the hall. They all walked home together. Marie saw Chris with his parents; she waved to him and he waved back. "See you tomorrow at your house," he called. "Your mom's invited us all."

"Great! Look forward to it!" Marie called back happily. She loved Christmas Eve. In Poland it was the main celebration—families got together to eat delicious food and open their presents. With her new friend joining them it was going to be extra special. She just wished her dad could be there, too.

She and Starshine were almost home now. Her mom and grandparents had just gone inside when the magic reindeer gave an excited little snort and looked up at the sky.

Marie did the same. She gasped as she saw the sight she'd been hoping for and dreading at the same time: a silvery line of shining reindeer hoofprints soaring overhead.

She froze. Starshine's White Crystal Herd was here. There was no mistake.

Starshine leaped out of Marie's bag with a flash of gold and silver light. He stood there as his real magical princely self: a young pure-white reindeer, with shining golden antlers and hooves. There was a halo of bright light all around him and gold dust gleamed in his fur.

"Starshine!" Marie gasped at his

regal beauty, blinking hard. She'd almost
forgotten how marvelous he looked
surrounded by that dazzling glow. "You're
leaving right now, aren't you?" she asked,
her voice breaking.

Starshine's chocolate-brown eyes lost a

little of their twinkle as he smiled sadly. "I must if I am to catch up with my father, Dazzler, Moonfleet, and the others."

A deep sadness washed over Marie, but she knew that Starshine had to leave and that she must be brave. She threw her arms around his shining neck. "I'll never forget you!"

Starshine allowed her to hug him one more time and then gently pulled away. "Farewell, Marie. I will not forget you, either," he said in a soft velvety voice. "Have a wonderful Christmas!"

The snow globe glowed brightly and a fountain of silver and gold sparkles sprinkled around Marie and tinkled as they hit the ground. Starshine leaped up into the sky; he faded and was gone.

Marie stood there with tears

pricking her eyes. She knew she would always remember the amazing adventure she and Starshine had shared. Something cold brushed her skin. It had begun to snow.

Marie looked up into the sky with delight. Snowflakes were falling thick and fast. She heard her mom calling her from inside the house. She was just about to go in when something made her look over her shoulder.

A familiar figure was walking toward her.

It couldn't be. Could it?

Marie blinked away the snowflakes on her eyelashes as a surge of pure happiness glowed through her.

"Dad! Oh, Dad! It's really you!"

Laughing and crying at the same time,

she flew toward him and threw herself
into his arms. He gave her a big hug.
"Hello, angel," he said in English.

He took a present wrapped in sparkly
paper out of his pocket. "Open it now.
This one's special."

Marie tore open the wrapping and
looked at a tiny snow globe in wonder.
Inside was a tiny white reindeer with lots

of other reindeer around him.

"I'm glad you made it home safely, Starshine!" she whispered. "Thank you for being my friend."

A white Christmas kitten needs a friend!

Magic Kitten

A Christmas Surprise

SUE BENTLEY

To Tibby, my fondly remembered marmalade sweetie

Magic Kitten

A
Christmas
Surprise

SUE BENTLEY

illustrated by Angela Swan

★ Prologue ★

Dust swirled around the young white lion's paws as he raced through the valley. Flame knew he shouldn't risk being out in the open. What if his uncle Ebony saw him?

Suddenly, Flame heard a terrifying roar as an enormous black adult lion burst out from behind some trees. The lion bounded toward Flame.

"Ebony," called Flame.

Flame leaped into the grass to hide. A bright white light flashed in the air and suddenly Flame had turned into a tiny,

snowy-white kitten with a fluffy tail.
The magic had worked again!

Flame's heart thudded in his tiny
chest as he edged backward to where
the grass grew thicker. His uncle Ebony
was very close. Flame hoped this
disguise would protect him, as it had so
many times before.

Flame heard a rustle in the grass and
a dark shape pushed toward him. Flame
was ready to fight. His emerald eyes
sparkled with anger and fear.

"Stay there, Prince Flame. I will
protect you," growled a deep but gentle
voice.

Flame meowed in relief as an old gray
lion peered down at him.

"Cirrus. I am glad to see you again. I

had hoped that by now, Ebony would be ready to give back the throne he stole from me," Flame said.

Cirrus shook his head. "That will never happen. Your uncle is determined to rule in your place. He sends spies to search for you. It is not safe for you to be here. Use this disguise and go back to the other world to hide."

The tiny kitten bared his sharp teeth as he looked up into Cirrus's face. "I wish I could fight him now!" Flame cried.

Cirrus's eyes flickered with affection. He reached out a huge paw and gently pet Flame's tiny fluffy white head.

"You are brave, Prince Flame. But now is not the time. Come back when you are stronger," Cirrus said.

Suddenly, Cirrus and Flame heard another roar from nearby. The ground shook as huge paws pounded through the tall grass.

"You cannot hide from me, Flame!" roared Ebony.

"Save yourself, Prince Flame. Go quickly!" Cirrus said.

Sparks glowed in the tiny kitten's silky white fur. Flame meowed as he felt the magic building inside him. He felt himself falling . . . the magic was working.

Chapter
ONE

"I really hope it's going to be a white Christmas!" Molly Paget said, peering hopefully out of the window. She sighed as raindrops snaked down the glass and blurred her view of the street outside. "Oh, well. There's still a week to go."

Molly jumped down the stairs two at a time and went into the kitchen where a delicious spicy smell filled the air. Her mom was just taking a tray of muffins out of the oven.

Mrs. Paget looked up and smiled. "I heard you running down the stairs. What's the hurry?"

Molly grinned. "There isn't one. I'm just in a good mood. Can I have one of those muffins?"

Her mom nodded. "Of course you can. Take one of those on the plate, they're cooler."

Molly picked up a muffin and took a bite. "Mmm, yummy. Tastes Christmasy!"

Her mom smiled. "I'm glad it passes the Molly test!"

"When are Gran and Gramps arriving?" Molly asked, munching.

Her grandparents lived near the coast. She hadn't seen them since the summer, but they were going to spend Christmas at Molly's house. Molly's eyebrows dipped in a small frown as she remembered how during the last visit to her grandparents' house, she had had to take her shoes off before going into the living room. Everyone always sat at the table to eat and no one was allowed to watch TV during the day. Molly hoped Gran would be less strict this Christmas.

"They'll be here the day before Christmas Eve," her mom said, wiping her hands on her apron. "I've still got desserts to make, a cake to ice, and tons of presents to buy. And we haven't even started clearing out the spare bedroom." A worried look came over her face. "Your Gran's great, but she has very high standards."

Tell me about it, Molly thought. "I'll help you. I'm good at clearing up and stuff," she said brightly.

"It's nice of you to offer, but Molly

and the word *help* can sometimes spell trouble!" Mrs. Paget said wryly, ruffling her daughter's blond hair. "I'll get your dad to give me a hand with the bedroom. It's his parents who are staying, after all."

"Did I hear my name?" Mr. Paget said, coming into the kitchen. His hair was speckled with dust and there were cobwebs sticking to his blue sweater. He quickly washed his hands before helping himself to a muffin.

"Da-ad! You've got yucky stuff all over you," Molly said, laughing. She reached up to pick off a cobweb.

"Do I? I didn't notice," Mr. Paget said around a mouthful of muffin. "I was just in the attic. I had to move a mountain of old stuff to get to the Christmas tree and decorations. Anyway, I found them in the end. They're in the living room."

"Great!" Molly said excitedly, already speeding out of the kitchen. "I'm going to put the tree up right now!"

"Slow down, Molly!" her mom called after her.

But Molly had already left. Mr. Paget shook his head slowly. "Molly's only got two speeds. Fast and faster!" he said as he followed his daughter.

By the time her dad came into the living room, Molly had her arms full of folded, green spiky branches. "There's an awful lot of tree," she said, peering into the long box. "I don't remember it being so huge."

Mr. Paget laughed. "Well, it couldn't have grown since last year, could it, you silly? I'll get the stepladder."

"That's a job well done!" Mr. Paget said an hour later.

Molly looked up at the Christmas tree, which almost touched the living-room ceiling. "It's impressive. I can't wait to decorate it!" She searched in another cardboard box and found some tissue-wrapped packages. Unwrapping one of them, she looked closely at the blue glass ornament. "Isn't this pretty? It's got silver-frosted snowflake patterns all over it," she said delightedly. "Do we have any more like this?"

Her dad nodded. "There are lots of them. I remember them hanging on our Christmas tree when I was little."

"Really? They must be ancient then," Molly said.

Mr. Paget grinned, giving her a playful nudge in the arm. "I forgot we had those ornaments. Be very careful with them."

"I will," Molly promised, unpacking the precious ornaments very gently.

Mr. Paget peered into the empty cardboard box. "That's funny. I thought the tinsel and other stuff was in there, too. Maybe it's in the garage. I'll go and look."

Molly frowned. She knew that her dad couldn't resist cleaning when he was looking for things. He would take forever. "Aw, do you have to do it now, Dad?"

Mr. Paget grinned at the look on her face. "Impatient to get going, aren't you? Why don't you start on the bottom branches? But you'd better wait for me to come back before you do the higher ones."

"Okay!" Molly said, already tearing open a packet of little green plastic hooks.

As soon as he'd left, she began hanging ornaments on the tree. Soon, the bottom branches were finished. Molly stood back to admire the way

the blue, red, and gold glass gleamed
prettily against the dark green.

Her dad still hadn't come back.
Molly looked longingly up at the
higher branches. She shifted her feet
impatiently. "Come on, Dad, you
slowpoke," she grumbled. She hesitated
for a minute and then dragged the stepladder closer to the tree.

He was bound to be back in a
minute. She'd just start doing a few
more branches. Climbing halfway up
the ladder, she began hanging
ornaments on the branches that were
within easy reach.

This is easy, she thought. *I don't know
what Dad was worrying about.*

She climbed higher to hang more

decorations. At this rate, she'd have the whole tree finished soon. At the top of the ladder, Molly leaned out farther to try and reach a branch near the top of the tree that would look perfect with the ornament she was holding.

And then she felt the ladder wobble.

"Oops!" Throwing out her arms, Molly tried to grab something to steady herself, but her fingers closed on thin air. She lost her balance and banged against the tree. It shook wildly and decorations began falling off in all directions.

Molly heard the precious ornaments smash into tiny pieces as they hit the carpet. "Oh, no!" she cried.

She looked down as she swayed

sideways, and then everything seemed to happen at once. The ladder and tree both tipped sideways and started to fall to the ground.

"He-elp!' Molly croaked, tensing her whole body for the painful bruising thud as she hit the carpet.

Suddenly, the room filled with a dazzling white flash and a shower of silver sparks. Molly felt a strange warm tingling sensation down her spine as she fell. The air whistled past her ears. There was a sudden jolt, but no hard landing.

To her complete shock, Molly was hovering in midair half a foot above the carpet. Swirling all around her was a snowstorm of brightly sparkling glitter!

She gasped as she felt herself turning
and then drifting gently down to the
carpet where she landed on her behind
with barely a bump. The sparkling
glitter fizzed like a firework and then
disappeared.

Molly sat up shakily and looked
around.

The ladder was upright and the tree was straight and tall once again. The delicate glass ornaments were all unbroken and hanging back in place on the branches.

But . . . I heard them smash! I don't get it . . . Molly said to herself. What had just happened? She felt like pinching herself to see if she was dreaming.

"I hope you are not hurt?" meowed a strange little voice.

Molly almost jumped out of her skin. "Who said that?" She twisted around, her eyes searching the room.

Crouching beneath the Christmas tree, Molly saw a tiny fluffy snow-white kitten. Its silky fur seemed to glitter with a thousand tiny, diamond-bright sparkles and it had the biggest emerald eyes she had ever seen.

Chapter
TWO

Molly's eyes widened. She must be more confused and shaken up by her fall than she'd thought. She'd just imagined that the kitten had spoken to her!

She looked at the kitten again and now its silky white fur and bushy tail looked normal. Perhaps it had wandered in when her dad left the door open on his way to the garage. "Hello. Where'd you come from?" she said, kneeling down and reaching a hand toward it.

"I come from far away," the kitten meowed. "When I saw you fall I used my magic to save you. I am sorry if I startled you."

Molly gasped and pulled her hand back as if she had been burned. "You . . . you can talk!" she stammered.

The kitten blinked up at her with wide green eyes. Despite its tiny size, it didn't seem to be too afraid of her. "Yes. My name is Prince Flame. What is yours?"

"Molly. Molly Paget," Molly said. Her mind was still whirling and she couldn't seem to take this all in. But she didn't want to scare this amazing kitten away, so she sat back on her heels and tried to stay as small as possible. "Um . . . I

don't know how you did it, but thanks
for helping me. I could have hurt
myself badly."

"You are welcome," Flame purred,
and his tiny kitten face took on a
serious look. "Can you help me, Molly?
I need somewhere to hide."

"Why do you need to do that?"
Molly asked.

Flame's emerald eyes lit up with anger. "I am heir to the Lion Throne. My uncle Ebony has stolen it and rules in my place. He wants to keep my throne, so he sends his spies to find me."

"*Lion* Throne?" Molly said doubtfully, looking at the tiny kitten in front of her.

Flame didn't answer. He backed away from the Christmas tree and before Molly knew what was happening, she was blinded by another bright silver flash. For a moment she couldn't see anything. But when her sight cleared, the kitten had gone and in its place a magnificent young white lion stood proudly on the carpet.

Molly gasped, scrambling backward on her hands and knees. "Flame?"

"Yes, it is me, Molly," Flame replied in a deep velvety roar.

Molly gulped, just getting used to the great majestic lion, when there was a final flash of dazzling light and Flame reappeared as a silky white kitten.

"Wow! I believe you," she whispered. "That's a cool disguise. No one would ever know you're a prince!"

Flame pricked his tiny ears and started to tremble. "My uncle's spies will recognize me if they find me. Will you hide me, please?"

Molly reached out and pet Flame's soft little head. He was so tiny and helpless-looking. Her soft heart melted. "Of

course I will. You can live with me. It'll
be great having you to cheer me up if
Gran gets in one of her grumpy moods.
I bet you're hungry, aren't you? Let's go
and find you some food."

Flame gave an eager little meow.

"Find who some food?" said her dad, coming into the room with a big cardboard box in his arms.

Molly jumped up and turned to face him. "Dad! Something amazing just happened. I almost fell off the ladder . . . I mean . . . er . . ." she stopped guiltily, deciding that it might be smart to skip that part. "I've just found the most amazing kitten and I'm going to look after him. And guess what, he's magic and he can ta—" she stopped suddenly again as Flame gave a piercing howl.

"Flame? What's wrong?" Molly said, crouching down to talk to him.

Flame blinked at her and then sat down on the rug and began calmly washing himself in silence. Molly looked at him, puzzled. Why didn't he explain?

"You and your imagination, Molly Paget! A talking kitten?" Her dad shook his head slowly. "I don't know where that little kitten came from, but you should look outside and see if one of the neighbors is looking for him!"

"No, they won't be . . ." Molly started to say, but she saw Flame raise a tiny paw and put it to his mouth, warning her to keep quiet. "I'll go check on the neighbors," she finished quickly. She picked Flame up and went into the front garden. "What was all that about back there?" she asked him once they were alone.

"I did not have time to explain before your father came in that you cannot tell anyone my secret," Flame meowed softly. "You must promise, Molly."

"Oh, no!" Molly's hands flew to her mouth. "But I almost told Dad everything. Have I already put you in danger?"

Flame shook his head. "No, it is okay. He did not believe you. Luckily, grown-up humans seem to find it difficult to believe in magic."

Molly breathed a huge sigh of relief as she looked into Flame's serious little face. "I promise I'll keep your secret from now on. Cross my heart and hope to die."

Flame nodded, blinking at her happily.

"I guess we should go and pretend

to look for your owner. Come on," Molly urged.

"So we'll just have to keep Flame . . ." Molly finished explaining as she faced her mom half an hour later. Flame nestled in her arms, purring contentedly.

Mrs. Paget was putting things in the dishwasher. She stood up and reached out to pet Flame's soft little white ears. "Oh, dear, we hadn't planned on having a kitten, especially with your grandparents coming. But if you've asked all around . . ." she said uncertainly.

"Oh, I did. I went to *dozens* of houses and no one knew anything about a white kitten," Molly lied. "So—can I open a can of tuna for Flame?"

Her mom smiled. "Sure. He's really gorgeous, isn't he? And I like his name. But I think that you might have to keep Flame in your bedroom while your Gran's here."

Molly frowned. "Why? What does she have against kittens?"

Mrs. Paget smiled. "It's not just kittens, it's pets in general. She won't tolerate hair on the furniture. As for muddy paw prints, wet fur, fleas—should I go on?"

"Flame doesn't have fleas!" Molly exclaimed. "Anyway, once Gran meets him I bet even she's going to love him, too. He's the cutest kitten ever."

"I agree with you. But I wouldn't be too sure that your gran will," her mom

warned gently.

Molly hardly heard her. "Come on, Flame, let's go and tell Dad that Mom says you can stay." Flame looked up at her and gave an extra loud purr.

Chapter
THREE

"It's the last day of the semester, so we'll be just doing fun stuff at school instead of lessons," Molly said to Flame as she pulled on her coat a couple of days later.

Flame had followed her into the hall, his fluffy white paws padding on the carpet.

"I have to hurry and catch the bus now, so I'll see you later," Molly said, bending down to pet him. "I really love having you living here and I wish you

could come with me, but we aren't
allowed to bring pets to school."

"But I can come!" Flame told her
with a happy little meow. "I will use
my magic to make myself invisible.
Only you will be able to see and hear
me."

"Really? That's *so* cool!" Molly said happily. "Okay then. Quick, can you get into my backpack before Mom and Dad see you and say you can't come with me?"

Flame nodded and jumped inside.

It was a short bus ride to school. Molly put her bag on her lap, so Flame could poke out his head and look at the brightly decorated stores and the big Christmas tree in town. Fairy lights glinted in the trees lining the streets and more colored lights were strung outside the big stores.

Flame's green eyes grew round with wonder. "I have never seen so many bright lights. They are like glowworms in a field of grass," he meowed.

"It's because of Christmas," Molly explained in a whisper. "The shops are full of presents and stuff and special treats."

Flame put his head on one side. "What is Christmas?"

"Oh, I forgot. I guess you don't have that in your world, do you?" Molly said. "Christmas is a special time, when the family gets together to celebrate the baby Jesus being born. We sing carols and give each other presents and eat lots of delicious food until we feel like bursting." She grinned.

Flame looked a bit confused. "It sounds very strange, but I think I will like Christmas."

Molly smiled. She decided to buy

him a really special present and put it under the tree for him to unwrap on Christmas morning.

The bus stopped outside the school. Molly got off and put her bag on her shoulder as she walked toward the school gate. A thin, pretty girl with long blond hair came running up. It was Shona Lamb, one of the most popular girls in Molly's class.

"Hey, Molly!"

"Hi, Shona!" Molly replied. She noticed that Shona was wearing some fabulous new boots. "Wow! When did you get those?" she asked admiringly. The boots were like the ones Molly wanted for Christmas, only more expensive-looking.

Shona glanced down at her cool boots. "What? Oh, yesterday. I'd forgotten about them already. But listen, I am *so* excited! I bet you can't guess what Mom's going to buy me for Christmas!"

Molly pretended to think hard. "A

sports car, a trip around the world, your own private plane?" she joked.

"Very funny. You're a riot!" Shona said, rolling her eyes. "It's a pony! I'm starting riding lessons soon. You'll be able to come over and watch me ride my very own pony!"

"Um . . . yes," Molly murmured, imagining Shona prancing about and showing off. *Just what I'd love to do. Not!* she thought.

Shona flicked her long blond hair over her shoulder and turned to another girl. "Hi, Jane! You'll never guess what I'm having—"

"As if we care!" whispered a disgusted voice at Molly's side as Shona and the other girl walked away together.

Molly turned and grinned at her best friend. "Hi, Narinder."

Narinder Kumar had an oval face and big dark eyes. Her shiny black braids reached down to her waist and her eyebrows were drawn together in a frown. "Sorry, but I can't stand Shona Lamb. She's so spoiled!"

"She can be a little annoying," Molly agreed. "But I don't mind her. Listen, there's the bell."

In the classroom, Molly opened her backpack so Flame could jump out. He gave himself a shake and then began washing. Molly knew that Flame was only visible to her, but she couldn't help looking around nervously. When no one seemed to notice Flame, though, she relaxed.

The teacher took attendance. Everyone answered as their names were called. ". . . Molly Paget," called Miss Garret.

There was no reply.

"Molly?" Miss Garret said again.

Narinder nudged Molly. "Miss Garret's calling your name."

Molly did a double take. She had been watching Flame leap from desk to desk, his bushy white tail streaming out behind him. "Sorry! Here, Miss Garret!" she shouted.

"Thank you, Molly," Miss Garret said patiently. She finished the attendance list and put it away before speaking to the class. "Now, everyone, we won't be

doing any schoolwork today. We're all
going to watch the younger children
perform their Christmas play in an
hour, so we've got just enough time for
a quick clean up."

When Molly, Narinder, and everyone
else groaned Miss Garret smiled.

"Cheer up! It won't take long. Abi

and Heather, would you organize the bookshelves . . ." She began giving out jobs to the class, ". . . And Molly and Narinder, perhaps you could clean up the art stuff, please?"

"Okay, Miss Garret!" Molly jumped up helpfully.

She and Narinder arranged the paper, paints, and brushes. Molly spotted a big

spray can of fake snow on a high shelf.
"Hey, look at this. I've got a great idea."

"What are you going to do?"
Narinder asked.

"Wait and see!" Molly slipped the can
under her school outfit.

While Narinder was putting the last
few things away, Molly wandered across
to the window where Flame was
curled up.

"What is that? Is it something nice to
eat?" the tiny kitten meowed eagerly.

"No, it's fake snow," Molly whispered.
"I'm going to spray snowflakes on the
window as a surprise for everyone."

Flame blinked at her. "What is
snow?"

Molly looked at him in surprise—

maybe it didn't snow where Flame came from. "It has to get very cold and then rain freezes in pretty patterns and white snowflakes float down from the sky. It's so beautiful," she explained. "I'm really hoping for a white Christmas."

Flame's emerald eyes widened in astonishment. "Snow comes from the sky? I would like to see it very much."

"I'll show you what it looks like!" Molly held the can up to the window and gently pressed the button. Nothing happened, so she shook the can hard and then tried again. Just then, someone tapped her on the shoulder.

"Molly, have you—" Shona began.

Molly lifted her finger as she turned

around, but a blast of white foam shot out with a loud whooshing sound. "Oh, no! The button's stuck!" she gasped, trying to free the nozzle.

Shona gave a loud shriek as a powerful jet of fake snow shot all over her clothes.

Chapter
FOUR

Molly finally managed to stop the can from spraying. She stared at Shona in horror.

A thick layer of fake snow covered her from her neck to her waist. It was dripping off the ends of her long blond hair and splatting onto the floor in soggy white blobs.

"Um, sorry . . ." Molly said lamely.

"I can't believe what you've done!" Shona howled. "Look at my hair! It's ruined!"

There were muffled giggles from Narinder and some other girls, but Molly didn't laugh. She felt terrible.

Miss Garret hurried over and began mopping up the sticky mess with handfuls of paper towels. "Calm down, Shona, this stuff washes out." She turned to Molly. "Why were you messing around with that spray can?"

"I was going to make snowflakes on the windows, but the nozzle got stuck," Molly explained.

"Oo-oh, you liar!" Shona burst out. "She did it on purpose, Miss Garret! She aimed right at me and made a big long squirt! She's just jealous because I have new boots *and* I'm getting a pony for Christmas!"

Molly blinked at Shona in disbelief. "I couldn't care less about your lousy boots and your stupid old pony!"

"That's enough, both of you!" Miss Garret said, frowning. "I'll speak to you about this later, Molly. Come to the bathroom, Shona. We're going to have to wash your hair and clothes. The rest of you had better go into the hall. The play's about to begin."

Molly hung back as Miss Garret and Shona and most of her classmates filed out. "Can I help it if the spray can decides to malfunction?" she said to Flame.

"It was very bad luck," Flame meowed sympathetically. "I am sorry that I could not use my magic to help you."

"That's okay. I know you couldn't give yourself away," Molly said.

Narinder ran up, grinning widely. "That was *so* hilarious! Serves that snobby Shona right. Stick to your story about spraying her accidentally and you'll be okay!"

"But it really was an accident," Molly protested.

"Yeah, right!" Narinder said. "I'm going to the bathroom. See you in the hall."

"But . . ." Molly gave up. "Come on, Flame," she whispered, shrugging. "I bet you've never seen a school play." As she went into the hallway, Flame scampered along at her heels.

Molly almost bumped into two older girls who were waiting just outside the classroom. She recognized them as Alice and Jane, two girls from the class above hers. They both lived near Shona and often hung out with her.

Alice was tall and thin and Jane was smaller with glasses.

As Molly went to walk past, Alice stuck out a skinny leg, so Molly almost tripped. "Oops. Sorry. It was an accident," she sneered.

"Yeah! Like what you did to Shona," Jane piped up, glaring at Molly through her glasses. "You'd better watch your back."

"Whatever!" Molly said, shrugging, but her heart beat fast as she walked quickly away from the bigger girls.

Molly tried to enjoy the school play. The younger kids were really cute in their angel wings and tinsel halos, but Alice and Jane's threat was still on her mind.

The rest of the day seemed to drag and Molly only managed to eat a tiny bit of her lunch, even though it was turkey with all the trimmings. The moment the school bell rang, Molly headed for the coatroom.

"Come on, Flame, can you quickly jump into my bag again? We don't want to bump into those two mean girls!" she urged.

She said a hurried good-bye to

Narinder at the gate. "Sorry I'm in such a rush. I've . . . er . . . got to hurry home today," she stuttered. "I'll call you!"

Narinder looked surprised. "Okay. See you!" she said, waving.

To Molly's relief, the bus was waiting at the bus stop. She managed to jump onto it, just before it pulled away. She got home safely and was hanging her

backpack in the hall when her mom
appeared from upstairs.

"Hello, love. You look upset. Is
something wrong?" Mrs. Paget asked.

"I . . . um, had a little accident,"
Molly began. She told her about
spraying Shona. "And everyone thinks I
did it on purpose!"

"But of course you didn't!" Mrs.
Paget said indignantly. "You sometimes
act without thinking first, but you don't
have a mean bone in your body!" She
gave Molly a hug. "Don't worry about
it. It'll all be forgotten about by next
semester."

"Do you think so?" Molly asked,
biting her lip.

"Definitely," Mrs. Paget said firmly.

She turned toward the plain white Christmas cake on the kitchen table. Icing pens, food coloring, and icing lay next to it. "How would you like to decorate the cake for me? I was about to start it, but I really need to run out to the store."

"Cool!" Molly said, immediately cheering up. "Just leave it to me, Mom!"

As soon as she'd waved good-bye to her mom, Molly came back into the kitchen and began making a robin out of icing. Flame sat on a kitchen chair, watching in fascination as she put the robin on the cake and then made squiggly lines with the icing pens.

Molly looked down at her work so

far. "Not bad. But it needs something else," she said, frowning. "I know! I'll make a snowman. I wonder if Mom's got any of that white ready-made icing stuff left."

Climbing onto a kitchen chair, she peered into the cabinet above the table. She stood up on her tiptoes and poked around behind a stack of cans. "I can't see any—"

"Look out!" Flame meowed warningly as Molly's elbow brushed against the cans.

It was too late. Three heavy cans fell out and landed right on the cake. *Thud!* The cake broke apart and icing and pieces of cake shot all over the table.

"Oh, no!" Molly groaned in dismay.

Flame stood up on his back legs
and rested his front paws on the table.
"Do not worry, Molly. I will help you,"
he purred.

Molly felt a warm tingling down her

spine as bright sparks ignited in Flame's silky white fur and his whiskers crackled with electricity. He lifted a tiny glittering white paw and sent a laser beam of silver sparks toward the ruined cake.

As Molly watched, the sparkling beam moved back and forth, forming the cake back into shape from the bottom up. "Wow! It's just like watching special effects in a sci-fi movie!" she said delightedly.

The cake was half-fixed again, when Flame's sparkling ears twitched. "Someone is coming!" he warned.

A second later, Molly heard the front door slam and voices echoed in the hall. "Hello, is anyone here? Surprise,

surprise!" called Gran Paget.

"Oh, no!" Molly gasped in panic, jumping down from the chair. "What's she doing here? Do something, Flame!"

Chapter
FIVE

Flame's whiskers crackled with another bright burst of power.

As Molly watched, everything went into fast forward. The laser beam whizzed back and forth, reforming the cake in triple-quick time. *Whump!* The cake plonked itself on the plate. *Whoosh!* The cans zoomed into the air. One, two, three—they stacked themselves in the cabinet. *Slam!* The cabinet door closed.

Just as the last fizzing spark faded

from Flame's white fur, Gran Paget
came into the kitchen. Gramps and
Molly's dad were with her.

"Gran! Gramps!" Molly cried, hugging
both of them.

"Hello, honey," Gramps said, kissing her cheek. "I bet you weren't expecting us, were you? We wanted to come a few days early to do some shopping and sightseeing. Your dad just picked us up from the train station."

"I wanted it to be a surprise. I don't know how I managed to keep it a secret," Mr. Paget said, grinning at his daughter.

A small flicker of unease rose in Molly's mind. "Er. . . Dad? Does Mom know about this?" she whispered to him.

"Not yet. But she's going to be delighted. I can't wait to see the look on her face!" he replied.

Neither can I, Molly thought,

remembering the state the spare room was in.

She heard the front door slam. "I'm back," called Mrs. Paget.

"Uh-oh," Molly breathed, running out to meet her mom and almost colliding with her. "Guess who's here! Gran and Gramps!"

Mrs. Paget almost jumped out of her skin. She dropped one of her bags and groceries began rolling everywhere. "Molly! Do you have to dart about like that?" she scolded.

"Oops, sorry!" Molly apologized, picking up the groceries.

Her dad and grandparents came out of the kitchen to help and soon everyone was laughing. Mrs. Paget hugged the grandparents. "What a lovely surprise," she said, looking hard at her husband.

"Time for a cup of tea and a muffin!" Mr. Paget said hurriedly.

"I'll fill the teapot," Molly said, rushing back into the kitchen.

Her mom followed her in. As she caught sight of the Christmas cake, she stopped dead. "Molly? Are you responsible for this?" she exclaimed.

"Um . . . yes. Sorry it didn't turn out very well . . ." Molly said over her shoulder. She was so grateful that Flame had put the cake back together in the nick of time that she had completely forgotten about the lopsided robin and messy squiggles of icing.

"But it's wonderful!" her mom said. "What a lovely snow scene, with a robin on a fence, and I love the snow kitten."

Snow kitten? Molly spun round.

A big grin broke out on her face as she saw that the cake was even better than before the cans had fallen on it. She bent down to look under the table where Flame was sitting. "Thanks, Flame," she whispered.

Flame winked at her and began purring loudly. Suddenly he gave a startled cry as a pair of arms shot under the table and grabbed him.

"How did that cat get in?" Gran scolded. "You're going outside, right now! Animals have no place in kitchens!" Before Molly could react, she opened the back door, threw Flame outside, and shut the door firmly.

Molly stared at her. "But it's cold out there! And Flame's only a tiny kitten!" she protested.

"He'll be fine. He's got a nice thick fur coat to keep him warm," Gran said, dusting off her hands.

Molly scowled. She marched across and opened the back door. "Flame's my kitten. If he has to stay outside, I'm staying with him!" she said stubbornly.

"Now, Molly. Don't be rude . . ." her mom warned gently.

"I don't care what anyone says!" Molly fumed. "I'll stay out here all night if I have to!" She picked Flame up and cradled him against her. She could feel him trembling. "Flame lives in the house. Tell her, Mom."

"Calm down, Molly. I think your gran thought Flame was just a stray who'd gotten in somehow. She didn't know you had a new kitten and I don't suppose your dad thought to tell her," Mrs. Paget said reasonably. She turned to Gran. "Molly's right. Flame

does live in the house. He's a very
clean kitten."

Gran straightened up her shoulders.
She didn't look pleased. "Have it your
way then, but I'm afraid I don't agree
with spoiling pets. They have to learn
their place."

Yes, and Flame's place is with me, Molly
thought. She stormed out of the
kitchen and hurried up to her bedroom
with Flame.

She curled up on her bed and lay
there cuddling Flame and feeling
miserable. Gran hated Flame. It was
unbelievable. How could anyone not
love her gorgeous kitten as much as
she did?

"It's not fair!" she complained, petting

Flame's fluffy white fur. "Now you'll have to be shut in my bedroom all the time Gran's here."

Flame's bright eyes sparkled with mischief. "I do not think so! Remember how I came to school with you. No one knew that I was there, did they?"

A slow, delighted grin spread across Molly's face. Of course, Flame could make himself invisible whenever he wanted to!

Molly awoke early the next morning and turned over to pet Flame, who was curled up beside her. *Strange,* she thought, *something seems different.*

"Listen? Can you hear anything?" she said to him.

Flame lifted his head and yawned sleepily. "I cannot hear anything."

"Exactly!" Molly cried. She jumped out of bed, threw open the curtains, and peered out of the window. "Oh! It looks so beautiful," she gasped.

The garden looked as if someone had thrown a thick white blanket over all of it. Snow had made bushes and flower beds into soft blurry humps.

Everything gleamed brightly under a clear silver sky.

"Hooray!" Molly did a little dance of happiness. "It *is* going to be a white Christmas this year! Flame! Come and look. It's been snowing all night."

Flame bounded across to the windowsill in a single leap. He stared out at the garden with shining eyes. "Snow is very beautiful," he purred happily, his warm kitten breath fogging the glass.

"Come on, Flame. I'm going to ask Mom and Dad if we can go sledding in the park!" Molly decided, already searching for a warm sweater and old boots.

She found her dad in the living room, finishing his breakfast cup of tea.

"Sledding in the park's a great idea," he said when Molly had finished speaking. "I'd rather come with you, but your Mom and I already promised to take Gran and Gramps for a walk around the big stores."

"Poor you!" Molly said, grinning at the look on his face. "Never mind, we can go sledding another day."

She was about to go out, when some new knitted cushions caught her eye. One had lime green and purple stripes and the other had orange and blue checks. "Wow! Where did those come from?" she asked.

"They were a present from your

gran. She's crazy about knitting," her dad said wryly. "They look . . . um . . . interesting with our red sofa, don't they?"

"Well, you can't miss them!" Molly burst with laughter. "I think I'll call Narinder and ask her if she wants to meet Flame and me at the park," she decided when she could speak again. "Have a nice time shopping, Dad."

"I'll try to," he said mournfully. "See you later. Come back home by lunchtime, sweetie."

"Okay," Molly answered, skipping into the hall.

Ten minutes later, she was bundled up in a warm coat, scarf, and gloves. "Come on, Flame. Let's go and meet 'Rinder," she said, opening the front door.

Flame leaped straight out and then gave a meow of surprise as he sank into the snow. He ran around, jumping sideways, and then he stopped to sniff at the snow. "It tastes delicious," he purred happily, nibbling at it.

Molly laughed as she watched him. Sometimes it was hard to remember that this cute playful kitten was a majestic lion prince. "It might be best if you ride on the sled," she decided.

"We'll get there faster and your feet will stay warm."

"My magic will keep me warm," Flame meowed, but he sprang onto the boat-shaped, red plastic sled like Molly suggested and settled down.

Molly set off, dragging her sled and Flame behind her.

The park was only a couple of minutes away. Lots of kids were already there. Some had sleds and others sat on garbage can lids or plastic bags as they slid down the snowy slopes. Molly saw Narinder waving as she came toward her. "Hi! Isn't this awesome!" she cried.

"Yeah! I love snow!" Molly said.

"Hey, I didn't know you had a kitten.

Isn't he gorgeous! Where did you get him from?" Narinder said, bending down to pet Flame's fuzzy little head.

Flame purred and rubbed against Narinder's gloved hand.

"I haven't had him long," Molly said quickly, hoping to avoid awkward questions. "Come on. Let's go sledding!"

She and Narinder trudged up the steep snowy slope with their sleds. At the top, Molly sat down and Flame jumped into her lap.

"I'll race you!" Molly said to Narinder.

"You're on!" Narinder shouted back. "Ready? One. Two. Three!"

"Hold on, Flame! Here we go!" Molly cried, pushing off with her hands.

Molly and Narinder flew down the slope, side by side. Flame's silky white fur blew back in the cold air.

"Whe-ee-e!" Molly yelled, grinning across at Narinder as her sled edged forward. "We're winning!"

Suddenly, near the bottom of the slope, she felt the sled skidding sideways. The front of it clipped a small bank of snow and it spun around and tipped over. Molly shot into the air and landed in the soft powdery snow with Flame still on her lap.

Narinder whizzed past, yelling triumphantly.

"Next time!" Molly shouted. Giggling, she started to get up. "Wasn't that awesome, Flame—"

"Well if it isn't that snob who sprayed stuff all over me in class!" said a voice. Shona Lamb stood there with her hands on her hips. She wore a pretty pink ski jacket and fluffy earmuffs. "Listen to her talking to her kitten. As if it's going to answer her!"

Molly's tummy felt queasy as she saw that Shona wasn't alone. Alice and Jane, Shona's mean older friends were with her.

Chapter
SIX

"Now you're in for it!" warned Shona, scooping up a big snowball.

"Yeah!" Jane said, bending down and making a snowball, too.

"Three against one isn't fair!" Molly said in a wobbly voice as she got to her feet. She quickly placed Flame on the sled out of harm's way. He stood there, tiny legs planted wide, his fur and bushy tail bristling with fury.

"Tough!" Alice said, grinning nastily.

Molly's mouth dried. Flame might want to help her, but he couldn't use his magic without giving himself away. Narinder was at the bottom of the long slope.

She was on her own.

A snowball hit Molly on the arm, but the powdery snow broke and it didn't really hurt. Another one landed on her back and then one hit her ear with a stinging blow. Molly hardly had time to make a snowball of her own and throw it, before she was hit again.

"Ow!" she cried as another snowball hit her neck and icy snow trickled inside her coat collar. "That's enough. You've paid me back," she said, trying not to cry.

"Maybe she's right," Shona said uncertainly. "Let's go."

"No, wait! I haven't finished with her yet!" Jane had a mean look on her face. She was patting her gloved hands together, making a snowball into a firm lump. Before Molly realized what she was going to do, Jane drew back her arm and aimed at Flame.

"No!" Molly screamed, throwing herself in front of him. The hard snowball smacked into her cheek with bruising force.

Molly gasped, stunned. Her cheek felt as if it was on fire and she felt sick and dizzy.

"Now you've really hurt her!" Shona said worriedly. "She's all white and shaky!"

Jane and Alice exchanged glances. "Run!" Jane said.

Shona came over to Molly. "Are you all right? I'm sorry. I didn't mean for it to go so far," she said, biting her lip.

"Just leave me alone," Molly murmured shakily.

As Shona ran after her friends, Molly's

legs gave way and she sank onto the
snow. Flame scampered up to her in an
instant. "Quick, Molly. Put me inside
your coat," he meowed urgently.

Molly did so. As soon as Flame was
hidden from sight, Molly heard a faint
crackling as sparks ignited in his fur,
and there was a soft glow from inside
her coat as Flame's whiskers fizzed with

power. The familiar warm tingling spread down her back and Molly felt a gentle prickling in her sore cheek. The pain drained away, just as if she had poured it down the sink.

"That's much better. Thanks, Flame," she whispered.

Flame touched her chin with his tiny cold nose. "You saved me from being hurt, Molly. You were very brave."

Molly's heart swelled with a surge of affection for him. "I'm not really. I just couldn't bear to think of anything happening to you. I love having you as my friend. I hope you can stay with me forever."

"I will stay for as long as I can," Flame purred gently.

"Molly! Are you all right?" Narinder's breath puffed out in the cold air as she came panting up the slope. "I feel awful. I saw those bullies coming at you, but I couldn't get to you quickly enough to help."

Molly grinned. "Don't worry about it, 'Rinder, it's hard to run uphill in the snow. Anyway, I'm okay. And I think they'll leave me alone now that they've gotten me back. Come on, let's go back up. I'm definitely going to beat you to the bottom this time!"

"Hi, we're home!" Molly sang out as she dumped her coat and boots and went toward the living room.

Her mom poked her head around the

door. "Shh. Can you be quiet, sweetie?
Gran's sleeping in there. We went on a
long hunt for some special knitting
wool and she's worn out. Did you have
a good time in the park?"

"Great, thanks. Where's Dad and
Gramps?" Molly asked.

"In the garage, messing around," her
mom replied. "They need a little relief
after all those stores! Lunch will be
ready soon, so don't go far. It's home-
made tomato soup."

"Sounds good." Molly went quietly into the living room and sat on the sofa to read a magazine. "There's no need to become invisible, Flame. Gran's asleep. Listen!" she whispered, giggling.

Soft snores rose from the corner chair, where Gran was asleep with her knitting bag in her lap. As Molly watched, the bag slowly tipped forward and a ball of blue wool fell out and rolled across the carpet.

Flame couldn't resist. He gave a tiny eager meow and pounced on it. Play-growling and lashing his tail, he chased the ball of wool around the back of Gran's chair.

Molly bit back a burst of laughter as Flame reappeared with the ball of wool held proudly in his mouth. He tossed his head and the ball of wool tightened. Gran's knitting seemed to jump out of the bag. On the end of the ball of wool there was a half-finished, blue and white striped sock.

"Uh-oh. Now you've really done it!" Molly breathed. She crept forward to rescue the knitting. But it was too late.

Gran opened her eyes, yawned, and sat up. As she spotted Flame she gave a gasp of horror. "My knitting! You little menace! What have you done? Just wait

until I get my hands on you!"

Flame laid his ears back and yowled with panic. He tried to run away, but the wool was wound tightly around his legs, and he fell over his own feet.

Red-faced, Gran got up from the chair but Molly was already bounding across the room. She got to Flame first. "Stop moving," she scolded gently, untangling him as quickly as she could. "That's it! You'd better scoot! Gran's on the warpath!"

Flame didn't need telling twice. Flattening his ears, he zoomed out and ran upstairs. Molly picked up the mess of wool and knitting and handed it to Gran.

Gran had a face like thunder. "That

sock's ruined and I don't like the idea of using the wool again after that little beggar's been chewing it. Those socks were for your dad. I'll never have them finished for Christmas now. I told you that kitten would be nothing but trouble!"

"Sorry, Gran," Molly said in a subdued voice. *Why didn't Gran just buy socks, like normal people did, anyway?* she thought. "Flame didn't mean to be naughty. He was just playing."

"Soup's ready! Molly could you go and tell your dad and Gramps, please?" Mrs. Paget called from the hall.

"Will do, Mom. Phew!" Molly breathed gratefully, escaping as quickly as she could.

Chapter
SEVEN

Molly had Flame in her bag as she walked out to the car with her dad the following afternoon. It was the day before Christmas Eve and they were all going shopping at the Christmas market in the square.

"I've been meaning to say thank you to you and Flame," her dad said.

"What for?" Molly asked, puzzled.

"For saving me from having to wear blue and white striped socks!" he said, smiling.

Molly laughed and gave him a
friendly shove, and then her face grew
serious. "Gran was furious about having
her knitting ruined. I don't think she'll
ever like Flame now," she said sadly.

"Oh, you never know. Gran's bark is
worse than her bite," her dad said.

"Really?" Molly said. Then, seeing her grandparents coming out of the house, she quickly got into the car with Flame.

As her dad drove them all into town, Molly counted out her money. She had been saving it up for weeks and had enough to buy gifts for everyone—including Flame. It was exciting to think of all the lovely things she was going to buy.

The market was crowded and colorful. It was full of exciting stands, selling things from all around the world. Colored lightbulbs flashed on the huge Christmas tree and tinsel glittered under the streetlights. People wrapped in hats and scarves walked around carrying bags and lots of presents.

As Molly, her parents, and her grandparents strolled among the stands Flame popped his head out of her bag. His nose twitched as he enjoyed the smells of roasting chestnuts and hot spiced chocolate.

"Isn't this great?" Molly whispered to Flame, looking at some pretty silk scarves. "I'm going to buy one of these for Mom."

Flame didn't answer, but Molly was too busy to notice. She paused to listen to some carol singers holding lanterns, their sweet voices rising on the frosty air. At other stands, she bought lavender bags for Gran, a key ring for Gramps, and a new wallet for her dad.

"I'm doing really well with buying presents," she said, glancing down at Flame. But his head wasn't sticking up out of her bag. "Flame? Are you taking a nap?" She reached her hand inside the bag to pet him and her fingers brushed against a tightly curled up trembling little body. "What's wrong?" she asked in concern.

"My uncle's spies are here. I can sense them," Flame said softly. "I must hide!"

Molly's heart clenched with panic. Flame was in terrible danger. Her mind raced as she tried to decide what to do. There was no way she was letting anyone hurt Flame!

Suddenly she had an idea. "Don't

worry! We're leaving," she whispered to
Flame.

Spotting her parents at a nearby
cheese stand, Molly ran straight over.
"Can we go home?" she pleaded. "I feel
awful. I think I'm going to be sick!"

Gran and Gramps appeared, holding
some bags. "What's wrong?" asked
Gramps.

"It's Molly. She feels sick," Mr. Paget
answered.

"It's probably all the free samples
she's tried," Gran said. "I think she'll be
okay in a minute."

"No, I won't!" Molly insisted. She
felt desperate. Rolling her eyes, she
gave a loud groan and clutched her
tummy. "I think I'm dying! It'll be all

your fault if I collapse right here in the market."

Even Gran looked alarmed.

"Don't be so dramatic, Molly. It's only a little tummy ache," her dad said mildly, but he looked worried. "Perhaps we'd better take you home."

"We're almost finished shopping, aren't we? Let's all go back," Gramps said.

Molly could have kissed him. She flashed him a grateful smile and then remembered that she was supposed to be feeling sick.

As they all hurried toward the parking lot, she pet Flame's trembling little body. "Hang on! We'll be out of here soon," she whispered.

Molly didn't see the dark shadowy shapes slipping between the stands or the narrow cruel eyes that searched the crowded market.

"He is very close," growled a cold voice.

"Ebony will reward us well for finding the young prince," hissed the other spy.

"I'm being allowed to stay up late tonight. We're all going to midnight Mass at the church. You'll love it!" Molly said happily the following afternoon.

Flame was curled up on her blanket, surrounded by pieces of shiny wrapping paper, ribbons, and tape. He was back

to his normal self, now that the danger
from his uncle's spies seemed to be far
behind him.

Molly was wrapping her presents in
shiny wrapping paper. "I hope those
horrible mean cats keep on going until
they jump into the sea and sink! And
then you can stay with me forever," she
said to Flame.

Flame blinked up at her. "They may
come back and then I will have to

leave at once. Do you understand, Molly?" he meowed seriously.

"Yes," Molly answered in a small voice. "But I'm not going to think about that."

She finished wrapping her presents and putting bows on them. "I'll go and put them under the tree now," she said to herself.

Leaving Flame napping, she went downstairs into the living room. Gramps was reading a newspaper and Gran was knitting. She had started a new scarf in pink, brown, and yellow stripes.

There was the sound of voices from the kitchen.

"Hi, Gran. Hi, Gramps," Molly said, bending down to put her presents with the others. A sudden thought struck her. Surely there was one missing. "Oh, no," she gasped. "I've forgotten to buy one for Flame." In all the rush of getting Flame away from his enemies, she'd completely forgotten to get him a present.

"What's wrong, sweetie?" Gramps asked, looking up from his paper.

Molly told him. ". . . and Flame's
going to be the only one without a
present to open on Christmas morning,"
she finished glumly.

"Oh, that's a shame," Gran said.

Molly looked at her in surprise. It
sounded like she really meant it. "I'll
just have to go to the store and get
one. Maybe Dad will take me. I'll ask
him," she said on her way to the door.

"I think it's too late, dear," Gramps
said. "The stores all close early on
Christmas Eve."

"Oh, yes," Molly remembered with
dismay. She stopped and turned back
around. This was awful. What was she
going to do? Flame would have to go
without a present.

Gran looked thoughtful. "I've got an idea," she said, producing the scrap of blue and white sock from her knitting bag. "I think I could make this into a toy mouse."

"Do you mean it?" Molly looked at her gran. Maybe she *did* like Flame a little bit, after all. She flew over and gave her a huge hug. "That would be perfect! Thanks, Gran. You're the best!"

Chapter
EIGHT

Molly felt full of the magic of
Christmas as she walked into the church.
The ancient walls flickered with the light
of countless candles, and footsteps echoed
on the stone floor.

Even though it was long past Molly's
usual bedtime, she didn't feel tired.

Flame was in her bag. And it didn't
matter if everyone could see him. Animals
and their owners were all welcome for
the special Christmas Eve service.

"Isn't it gorgeous in here?" she

whispered to him, looking at the
candlelight flickering on the stained-
glass windows and the big vases of
flowers, holly, and ivy.

The church was packed and everyone

was in a good mood. There were hot
drinks, muffins, and bags of fruit and
nuts to snack on. A special band with
amazing instruments from all around
the world played and dancers performed
folk dances. And then the church choir
sang and everyone joined in with the
carols.

Molly caught sight of Shona with her
parents. She hesitated for a moment and
then waved at her. Shona looked
surprised and then she waved back,
smiling. "Merry Christmas!" she called.

"Merry Christmas!" Molly replied
happily.

"I got my pony. You'll have to come
over and see him. He's gorgeous,"
Shona said.

Molly bit back a grin. She was glad
they were friends again, but Shona
would never change.

After the service ended, Molly and
Flame, her parents, and grandparents
all trudged home through the snow. A
big silver moon shed its light onto the
glittering snow crystals on the ground.

Molly held her bag close to her chest,
so that she could pet Flame without
anyone noticing. "This has to be the
best Christmas Eve ever," she whispered
to him.

Just before she went up to bed, Gran
put a tiny package into her hand. "For
Flame. I hope he likes it," she said.

Molly threw her arms around her and
kissed her cheek. "I love you, Gran."

Gran's eyes looked moist and shiny. "I love you, too, Molly."

Molly slipped Flame's present under the tree before she went up to her bedroom. She felt so excited that she was sure she wouldn't sleep a wink. She'd just lie there in the dark, waiting for Christmas day.

After undressing and brushing her teeth, Molly slipped into bed. "Good night, Flame," she whispered, breathing in his sweet kitten smell as she cuddled with him.

Seconds later, she was asleep.

It felt like about five minutes later, when Molly opened her eyes. She was amazed to find the winter light pushing through her curtains.

"Come on, Flame. It's Christmas morning!" She leaped out of bed, threw her dressing gown on over her pajamas, and pushed her feet into her slippers.

She ran down the stairs two at a time, with Flame running at her heels.

"Merry Christmas!" she said, bouncing into the living room.

Her mom and dad and grandparents were already dressed and sitting with hot drinks. They looked up and smiled as Molly burst in.

"Merry Christmas, sweetie," said her dad, pouring more coffee.

"Merry Christmas," chorused her mom and Gran and Gramps.

"Can we open our presents now?" Molly said, going to sit cross-legged on the rug with Flame in her lap.

"We thought you'd never ask!" Gramps said. "We've all been waiting for you to wake up."

Molly unwrapped her presents eagerly. She had some books and music and lots of other cool stuff. But best of all were the new boots she'd been hoping for. "Cool! Thanks so much for my lovely presents, everyone!" she said, putting the boots on right away.

"Interesting look with those pajamas!" her dad joked.

Everyone laughed.

"Here's your present, Flame!" Molly loosened the wrapping paper.

He ripped it open with his sharp teeth and claws, a look of delight on his tiny face. The moment Flame saw Gran's knitted mouse, he gave an excited little meow. Grabbing it in his mouth he padded proudly around the room, his bushy tail high in the air.

"I'm glad someone likes my knitting!" Gran said, giving Molly's dad one of her looks.

Mr. Paget kissed Gran's cheek and then winked at Molly.

Molly choked back a laugh. "Flame adores his mouse, Gran! Um . . . is it okay if I call Narinder and ask if she wants to come and listen to my new CDs later on?" she asked.

"Of course it is," said her mom. "And

then can you hurry up and get dressed? Breakfast's almost ready. It's your favorite."

"Okay," Molly said, going out into the hall.

Suddenly, Flame streaked past her and raced upstairs so fast that he was a tiny white blur. Molly frowned. He'd never done that before.

"Flame? What—" she broke off as a horrible suspicion arose in her mind. She started running after him, her phone call forgotten for the moment.

As Molly reached the landing, there was a bright flash from her open bedroom door. She dashed into her room. Flame stood there, no longer a tiny kitten, but a magnificent young

white lion with a coat that glittered and
glinted with a thousand sparkles. An
older gray lion with a wise and gentle
face stood next to him.

"Prince Flame! We must leave now!" the gray lion growled urgently.

Molly caught her breath as she understood that Flame's enemies had found him again. This time he was going to leave for good.

Flame's emerald eyes crinkled in a fond smile. "Merry Christmas, Molly. Be well, be strong," he rumbled in a velvety growl as a whoosh of silver sparks spun around him. And then he and the old lion disappeared.

"Good-bye, Flame. Take care. I'll never forget you. I hope you regain your throne," Molly said, her heart aching.

Molly knew that she'd remember this Christmas forever. Having Flame as her friend, even for only a short time, was

the best present she would ever have.
She stood there for a moment longer as
she brushed away a tear.

And then she remembered Narinder.
As Molly went downstairs to phone her,
she found herself smiling.

About the
AUTHOR

Sue Bentley's books for children often
include animals, fairies, and wildlife.
She lives in Northampton, England, and
enjoys reading, going to the movies, and
watching the birds on the feeders outside
her window. She loves horses, which she
thinks are all completely magical. One of
her favorite books is *Black Beauty*, which
she must have read at least ten times. At
school she was always getting scolded for
daydreaming, but she now knows that she
was storing up ideas for when she became
a writer. Sue has met and owned many
animals, but the wild creatures in her life
hold a special place in her heart.

Don't miss these Magic Puppy books!

Don't miss these Magic Kitten books!

Don't miss these Magic Ponies books!

Don't miss these Magic Bunny books!